# *ROSCO JACK OF GATEWAY FARM*
# *"THE RETURN OF THE PIRATE"*

*A NOVEL BY*

*KEN BANGS*

Rosco Jack of Gateway Farm is a product of Ken Bangs Writing.

Fifth  Printing.

Rosco Jack is composed and edited in Grammarly Pro. It is printed in Cambria.

**Rosco Jack of Gateway Farm is dedicated to my beloved grandchildren, Miranda and K.W.**

**Rosco Jack of Gateway Farm**

~

***The Return of The Pirate***

## Foreword

Gateway Farm is a real place, just outside of New Boston, in the piney woods of East Texas. Ken and Trudy Bangs owned and operated Gateway for ten years.

Some of the events and characters of this story are real; some are fictional. All of the dogs, except Ginger, came to Gateway as castaways.

Some came with physical impairments resulting from beatings. Some were cast off after suffering injuries that rendered them incapable of returning to the pit as combatants in the illegal and cruel blood sport of dogfighting. Some were just not wanted.

At Gateway, they all were received with open arms, given the best care possible, and loved unconditionally.

This is the story of one of those castaways, Rosco Jack, a small Jack Russell terrier who was abandoned at the farm's front gate.

Surrounded by predators, he found a way to survive the night and greeted the dawn with his faith in mankind unshaken despite the actions of the one who had cast him aside.

Rosco teaches us the importance of managing our fear; that the possibilities of success remain as long as we refuse to give up, that it is important not to judge all by the actions of one, and the power of love in healing the past and establishing the future.

From Rosco, we learn the importance of accepting instruction from those whose life experiences have qualified them to teach, the need for each of us to accept who and what we are, the value of co-existing with our fellow creatures, and the power of recognizing and acting on the opportunities of life.

Rosco Jack of Gateway Farm is written for all of those who face adversity, struggle with personal fear, and dream of overcoming.

But most of all, Rosco the pup illustrates the power in refusing to give up.

**CONTENTS**

**Book Two ~ The Return of The Pirate**

## Cast Away

Mattie shifted as her pups nudged her, seeking to feed again. Eight weeks had passed since she'd given birth, and four of the six had stopped depending on her dwindling supply of milk, but the two smallest still pressed her. Lifting her head, she looked at these two, jostling for position and worried. Her mother's instinct told her they were at risk. The door opened, and light spilled across the porch.

"Hello, Mattie," the master spoke softly to her.

His voice was strained, and the hour was late. Mattie knew something was about to change. The man kneeled, rubbed her head, and spoke gently to her.

"Mattie, old girl, I hate to do this, but we can't keep these pups. I have found homes for four, but no one wants these two runts," he sighed.

He picked up the two wiggling pups, and they immediately started to cry out. Mattie stood, looking up at the master with begging eyes, but she knew he would not change his mind. The screen door banged as he stepped off the porch carrying her beloved puppies into the darkness.

The back door opened again, and the master's wife came onto the porch.

"Tom," she called, "are you sure about this? Those two pups won't be any trouble. I can't stand the thought of casting them away."

"Now, Wilma," Tom said. "We already have four dogs. Besides, these two are runts. They will never amount to anything. The choice is to knock them in the head or carry them off. Which do you want me to do?" he asked.

"Stop it, Tom," his wife cried. "There is no way I am going to allow you to kill those helpless puppies. Now you promise me that you won't hurt them and that you will drop them in a safe place. Near a house."

"Okay, Wilma. That is my plan," he said, thinking of the place he had already chosen.

Wilma turned, looked at Mattie with tears in her eyes, and walked back into the house.

Tom carried the pups to his car and placed them in a box on the front seat next to him. The puppies whimpered as Tom started the car and drove away with them.

Tom grumbled, "Danged pups. Soon as I can, I'm taking Mattie and Ralph into the vet and get them both fixed. Thank goodness Sally and Joe are past the point of having pups."

The little female was whimpering and trying to get out of the box. Finally, she tipped over the box and crawled onto Tom's lap. He looked down at the scrawny little thing. She crawled onto his leg, and stood with her front paws on his belly.

Tom reached down to move her away. As he picked her up, she licked his hand. He looked at her; and she met his eyes, wagging her tail. She whimpered a plea for mercy.

Tom dropped her back into the box, "Nope, my mind is made up. You both have to go," he said.

Tom kept his eyes on the road, refusing to look at the pups, but he could not shut out their cries. He knew their chance of survival would be slim. But his heart was hardened, and he drove on.

Ten miles down the highway, Tom turned from the pavement onto a dirt road. Giant old trees overhanging the roadway blocked the moon's light, deepening the darkness.

Ahead, Tom saw the farm. There were no lights on at this hour, but he had driven past it several times and knew it was large and well cared for. He slowed the car as he approached the farm's front gate. He turned his lights off, hoping not to be seen.

"Why do I feel so guilty about this?" he asked himself.

He turned onto the lane, opened his door, and set the pups on the drive. The little female cried out to him, licking his hand and trying desperately to get back in the car. He brushed her aside and closed the door of the car.

Tom backed out and drove away. He looked into his rearview mirror. The little female tried to follow him, chasing the car on weak legs. He watched her stumble and fall. She picked herself up, turned, and trotted back to where her brother sat, watching the car's lights disappear.

'*Strange,*' thought Tom. '*I might have misjudged that little male. He refuses to beg. He might make it, and if his little sister follows his lead, she might too.*'

Tom almost stopped, but then his hardness of heart overrode the flash of compassion, and he drove on into the night.

The pups were alone. They huddled together, shivering despite the hot August night. Their senses were alive to the smells and the sounds of much larger animals stalking the deep shadows cloaking the lane.

A light breeze stirred, bringing a heavy, musky smell. They found it familiar yet threatening. They knew the smell was that of a cat, but not like those they had encountered on the porch back home. This was the smell of the wild.

Leaves rustled, and the smell grew stronger. They heard soft, stealthy steps. They were those of an animal on the hunt. The pups knew they were the hunter's prey.

The little male saw one spot that was darker than the rest of the night surrounding them. He moved to it and found the hollow trunk of one of the giant trees.

Stepping in, he moved to the side and whimpered for his sister to join him. She followed, and they sat huddled together, waiting. The steps drew closer, and they heard the deep growl as the predator found their scent trail.

The little male moved back, into the deepest corner, and pressed his back against the trunk of the old tree.

He knew the cat would find them in the hollow, but he felt they would be out of his reach. It was a time that called for patient courage. They had to wait it out. He called for his sister to join him.

The little female whimpered. She looked back at her brother, but fear drove her out of their sanctuary. She bolted, running down the lane in the direction Tom took, after casting them away.

With a snarl, the big cat sprang from the shadows to overtake the little one. She yelped out her fear and pain. Then there was silence.

The male sat helplessly and watched the big cat carry the now limp body of his little sister into the deepness of the night. He knew that he must remain still, and quiet. Discovery meant death.

The heat was oppressive. His eyes grew heavy. Soon fear yielded to fatigue, and he slept.

He woke as the sun peeked over the pines to light the lane. He was alone.

The memory of the big cat came flooding back, and he began to shake. But then, he steeled himself. The cat was not here. The deep night had ended, and he was alive. He grieved for his sister, but he was determined to survive. He knew he had to move.

Instinct told him he had to find people. Even though Tom had cast him away, the pup knew mankind would provide protection from that which lurked in the darkness.

Looking back, he considered the road Tom had used to bring them to the farm. His heart told him there was no going back, so he turned in the opposite direction and hurried down the lane toward the houses in the distance.

His legs were short, and the distance seemed so great. He pressed on until he could go no more. Hunger and weariness pulled him down, and he slept again.

"Hey, look at this!" The sound of a voice awakened the pup. He looked to see a man stooping to pick him up. The man's touch was gentle, and the expression on his face brought the pup peace. The pup sensed that this man was safe. He wagged his tail and licked the hand that was caressing him.

"Well, little buddy looks like we have another castaway. Don't you fret. The Lord brought you to us, and this will be your home. Hey, Trudy, honey, come look what the Lord has brought us," the man called out.

The pup wiggled around at the sound of steps and saw the woman.

"Look at my little man. Aren't you just the cutest thing? Ken, what kind of puppy is he?" she asked.

Ken held him up and looked him over.
"Sugar, I do believe he is a little Jack Russell mixed up with some other Rosco breed of dog," Ken said.

The woman called Trudy reached for him and said, "A Jack Russell and a Rosco mix you say. How interesting," she said.

Looking at the puppy, she said, "I am going to call you Rosco Jack. That will be your name. Rosco Jack of Gateway Farm," the love in her voice brought him peace.

Her soft hands took him from the man, and she cradled him to her chest. Walking slowly and talking softly, she carried him into the house and out onto the back porch. She pulled a cushion from a chair and placed Rosco on it.

Rosco heard the door open again, and the heavy steps of the man came to him. He was holding a bowl, and Rosco's nose told him it was food. The man placed the bowl in front of Rosco, and Rosco buried his nose in a deep pool of cold milk. He lapped until his little belly would allow no more. Then he curled up on the pillow and slept.

Rosco dreamed. He was in the car again. *The door was opening. He watched as the man called Tom cast them out and then hurried away. He felt the fear as he and his sister realized they were alone.*

*They pressed together in the deep shadows, listening as the big cat searched for them. So different from the ones he had seen back home. Home. Mom. Would he ever see them again?*

*Then the cat was there, its' green eyes wide as it lunged forward. His sister yelped once and was gone, clutched tightly in the mouth of the big cat.*

Rosco woke, his heart aching for his sister. He sat up and looked around. It was dark and the night was once again filled with scary sounds and smells. He missed his mother and the safety he'd felt when pushing in against her soft, warm side. Overcome with sorrow, Rosco pointed his little nose to the sky and howled out his misery.

In the midst of his sorrow, Rosco was aware of footsteps coming towards him from within the house. The door opened, and light pooled around Rosco.

The master, the man the woman had called Ken, called to him softly, and Rosco scurried across the porch to sit at his feet.

Loving hands picked him up and cradled him, and the man spoke. Rosco did not know what he was saying, but he knew he was offering comfort. Ken placed Rosco on his pillow and rubbed his head. Rosco knew he had found a home and was safe here on the porch.

## The Pond

Rosco loved the porch. It was more than his safe place; it was where he met with Ms. Trudy and Ken, who he now considered his master. Each day they would bring him food, milk fortified with Karo Syrup at first, and gradually solid food.

They would sit with him as he ate, stroking him with gentle caresses and talking in soft tones that brought him peace. Rosco especially loved to have Ms. Trudy sit with him. He would drink his milk and then crawl into her lap and drift off to sleep with her telling him what a good boy he was.

Rosco had already sensed that these people were safe, but now their kindness caused his trust to grow. He came to love both of his people, and he knew they would protect him from harm. He was beginning to feel something growing in him, a need to protect them too.

Ms. Trudy had given him a rubber ball and some chew toys. During the long summer days, he would lie on his pillow chewing the toys or just watching the world go by. Each evening, as the sun set and darkness came to the farm, the master would close and lock the gate so that nothing could get onto the porch to harm Rosco. He understood what the master was doing and felt protected. Gradually, he stopped dreaming of the big cat.

Summer passed quickly. Each day brought a new adventure, and Rosco grew.

Then came the morning when the master came striding out with Ms. Trudy following closely behind him. Rosco could tell they were not in agreement on whatever they were talking about. There was tension in the air.

He thought back to that night when Tom had stepped onto the porch, and Rosco's life had changed forever. A change was coming again; he could feel it. But unlike that night with Tom, now Rosco felt no fear. These were his people, and he was their pup.

"Now, Ken," Ms. Trudy said. "I think you are moving too quickly here. Rosco is just a little man, and in no way is he ready for that pond. Why, there are fish in there big enough to eat him, not to mention the turtles and snakes."

"Ah, Sugar, stop your fretting. I'm going with him, and Ginger will be there too. He will be okay. Rosco can't spend his whole life tied to your apron strings. It's time for him to get off this porch. He needs to learn, and dogs learn best from other dogs. Now, just relax," Rosco heard the master say.

"Okay. But let me tell you one thing, Ken Bangs. If anything happens to Rosco, you head on to the barn because you will not get back into this house," Ms. Trudy said as she walked away.

"Wow, Rosco! I believe she means it. Still, it's time for you to experience life off the porch. Ginger, come here, girl," the master called.

Ginger climbed the steps and sat down in front of the master. She looked once at Rosco, then turned her face to look at the master and to wait for his commands.

"Good girl," the master said as he rubbed her head. "Now, girl, I need you to take this pup under your wing this morning and introduce him to the posse. Then I'm going to walk down to the pond, and I want you to bring him along so he can begin his orientation to Gateway Farm.

You watch him. If a turtle or, God forbid, Big Blue tries to pull him under, I depend on you to rescue him. Got it? Good. Let's go."

The master stepped down off the porch, and Ginger

followed. Rosco waddled over to the steps and looked down. Fear of the height pushed him back against the door, where he sat down and looked at the master.

"Come on, Rosco," the master coaxed. "Come on, big boy."

Ginger climbed the steps, nuzzled him with her nose, and then walked to the steps. She looked back at him and wagged her tail.

Rosco stood and approached the steps. Ginger took the first step, stopped, and looked back. Rosco lunged forward and tumbled all the way down. He landed on the sidewalk at the bottom of the steps, bounced, and rolled onto the grass.

The master was laughing, and all the other dogs were looking at him. Rosco rolled over and stood to study the pack. It was the first time Rosco had seen them all together.

Ginger Bear, the golden lab, was the biggest and oldest, thus the undisputed leader. Then there were Bo, Mercie, Gracie, and Collins. Ken called Collins "The Pirate" because he was always breaking the rules and trying to *'sail his own ship.'*

Rosco had heard Ken tell Ms. Trudy that there were now six dogs with Rosco, and he was thinking about naming the group "The Gateway Six Pack." Ms. Trudy didn't like that and said, "No, they should be called the Gateway Posse."

One by one, the posse sniffed and nuzzled Rosco. He sat quietly, enduring each inspection. Then came Collins. He sniffed Rosco, nudged him around a bit, then lifted his leg and peed on him.

Rosco was humiliated. A fury sprang up from deep inside the pup, and he leaped at Collins with a yelp, clamping his puppy teeth onto Collins's upper lip.

Collins cried out in pain and surprise. One short shake of his head and Rosco was sent bouncing across the yard. Collins pounced on him with the intent to teach the pup a lesson.

A blonde blur pushed Collins over onto his back. It was Ginger.

She stood over Collins for a minute until his anger subsided and then let him up. She turned, trotted over to Rosco, and sat down beside him, facing the rest of the posse. Ginger had spoken. Rosco was under her protection.

Once that was settled, Ginger led the posse to the pond. It was time for Rosco to start learning about life on the farm.

Rosco felt a wariness settle over the posse as they left the safety of the house. He struggled to keep up, and Ginger paused at the fence to wait.

The barbed wire presented no challenge to the big dogs, but to Rosco, it seemed impossible. The bottom strand was a good six inches off the ground. It was too low for him to crawl under without being struck by the sharp barbs and too high for him to step over without scraping his belly.

Ginger watched him as he ran up and down the fence, barking out his frustration. Then, taking him by the nape of the neck with her mouth, she picked him up and lifted him over the fence.

Rosco was embarrassed. He found facing the rest of the posse hard, so he sprang forward, racing headlong toward the pond.

He was at top speed as he ran up the ramp and onto the dock. He barely had time to realize his mistake before the dock ended, and he found himself in midair, dropping quickly into the water below. Rosco experienced the absence of the firm earth for the first time, and Panic sat in.

Rosco did not know if he was upside down or right side up. He could see nothing but darkness. There was a strange pressure in his ears, and his lungs were bursting for breath. All Rosco knew was that he wanted out of this unfamiliar environment.

Thrashing as fast as his four legs could move, Rosco broke through the surface and gulped the fresh air. He kept paddling and moved through the water toward the bank. His paws touched the bottom, and he ran out of the water and onto the solid earth. Rosco shook himself and sat down.

As he sat watching the other dogs swim, there was a swirl in the water, and a big blue fish came up. He had long whiskers on the sides of his face, big eyes, and a wide mouth. Out of that mouth came a stream of water directed at Rosco. It hit him full in the face. Sputtering and yelping, Rosco jumped back and started to bark at the fish.

Ken watched the interplay between the big blue fish and Rosco the pup. *'Good. Rosco needs to learn that Big Blue is not to be trusted and now is as good a time as any,'* he thought.

Big Blue was also watching Rosco closely. The pup's angry face amused the fish, but the squeaky puppy's voice also grated on his nerves. *'Hey! Kill the racket, Jack,'* the fish was thinking.

Blue, or Big Blue as he thought of himself, hated for the posse to swim in the pond. The other residents of the pond, he liked to think of them as his subjects, didn't like it either.

They looked to Blue to keep things in order. The swimming created waves and stirred up the water. It disturbed the peace of the pond.

Blue looked around and saw the eyes of his subjects above the water, watching to see what he would do about this intrusion into their home.

He glanced over at Ginger and the posse, swimming and splashing all across the pond. Once they were in the water, he was no longer the King of Gateway Pond. They were too big for him to pull under, and they swam wherever and for as long as they wanted.

*'But this pup is a different matter. He is so small that I can take him under if I can get him back into the deep water. That might make them think twice about barging into our home,'* Blue said to himself.

Rosco was no longer sitting. He was furious and had moved down to the water's edge. Ken watched as he edged closer and closer to the water, and then his two front paws were in the water.

Ken knew that Blue would take Rosco under if he got back in the water.

"Rosco, come on, boy," Ken called to the angry little pup.

Blue looked back at the barking pup. He turned and flipped his tail, spraying more water over the pup. That did it. Rosco charged toward the water.

"*ROSCO*," Ken yelled.

The pup stopped and looked back at Ken. Then he turned and trotted back to where his master stood.

"Good boy Rosco. Listen now; you have to control that anger. Uncontrolled anger will take you places you don't want to be, keep you longer than you want to stay, and cost you more than you are willing to pay. Don't let that happen," Ken patted Rosco.

*'Okay, so you escaped this time, Rosco. But you'll be back, and things will be different the next time,'* Blue smiled as he sank into the deep.

Ken walked toward the house, thinking as he walked. He had stood aside as Rosco had met the posse. He had remained quiet as Collins peed on Rosco, and he had been delighted to see Rosco's response.

*'Wow, I have me a special little dog here. There is something in this little man that sets him apart. He is a real overcomer who will refuse to allow his circumstances to set his course in life. I like this dog!'* Ken thought.

Ken played the morning's actions over in his mind. He remembered watching Rosco follow Ginger to the pond, seeing him become frustrated about being unable to get over the fence. Ken remembered Ginger lifting Rosco over the fence and how he had laughed when the pup's impatience led him to run forward, not knowing that the dock ended and the dark water waited. Rosco had learned the folly of running headlong into the unknown. Rosco had learned a *'deep'* lesson. Ken chuckled at his own humor.

Satisfied that all was well, Ken climbed the steps and onto the porch to get the dogs' breakfast set out.

Rosco heard a shrill whistle split the air, and Ken shout, "Breakfast, come and get it!"

In a blur, all the other dogs were out of the water and running towards the house. Rosco did his best to run, but he kept stumbling and falling.

Still in his mind's eye was Big Blue spitting on him. He felt the hair on the back of his neck standing up, and he felt a growl start to work its' way up from deep in his chest.

He wanted to turn and bark out his frustration, but by now, he could smell breakfast, and hunger overcame his rage.

The master was placing bowls full of food out for the dogs. Each dog had his own, except for Rosco. He sat down and barked at the master. The master laughed and picked him up.

"Hey, boy, I'm going to give you yours. But if I feed you here with the big dogs, they will eat theirs and then take yours away from you. So, up you go, onto the porch. Let me close the gate. Here is your milk and some scrambled eggs to go with it. Eat, boy."

Rosco was already eating up. He lapped the milk, and then he wolfed down the scrambled eggs. *So good!* Finished, he sat, licked his lips, and wagged his tail.

He heard a splash from the pond. He looked toward the sound and saw the big blue fish jumping high into the air and nosing over to re-enter the water with a splash. It was like he was once again showing Rosco that he was the King of the pond. Rosco could almost read the fish's mind, '*Yeah, that's right. Go ahead and wag your tail. Be a good dog. Me, I live by what I catch, and I rule the kingdom in which I live. That's the difference between a fish and a dog. No man pats my head.*'

Rosco was irritated. His ears perked, his tail stopped wagging, and the hair on the back of his neck stood up.

"That's right, Rosco. You've got him pegged. Big Blue is trouble. Stay away from him."

The master rubbed Rosco's head and walked into the house.

"Where is Rosco?" Ms. Trudy asked.

"He's just finished his breakfast and is resting a minute," Ken replied.

"Well?" she asked.

"Well, what?" Ken said.

"How did my little man do down at the pond?"

"Just fine. And I'll tell you another thing; there is something special about that dog. He has this ribbon of steel running through him. He will not be intimidated. He is an overcomer," Ken said. "You watch. He will become a full member of the Gateway Posse."

"Don't you get carried away," Ms. Trudy said. "He's still a puppy, and I do not want him hurt. Ken, a big hawk, could swoop down and carry him off. Promise me you won't let him get hurt."

"Okay, Sugar. You're right. He still has much growing to do. We'll leave him on the porch for now. Come fall or early winter, and we'll take a second look," Ken said.

"Does that mean that he stays on the porch for now?" Ms. Trudy asked.

"Yes, he does. For now, except when he is with me," Ken said.

## Red Demons

After breakfast, Ken climbed onto his golf cart. "Come on, Rosco!" Ken patted the seat next to him and called to the pup softly. "Come on, boy. Get in here with me. Go with me to water the new trees." Rosco jumped onto the seat, and Ken started the motor.

Ken shifted into gear, and the cart started moving slowly at first, then faster and faster. Rosco loved the wind in his face and being next to the master.

House to house they went. At each house, the master would get out and pour water on every tree and all the plants. Rosco followed him.

At one house, Rosco decided to scout out the trees ahead of the master. He ran to the first, lifted his leg, and peed. It felt so natural to him. Rosco scratched the grass, growled his puppy growl, and strutted to the next tree.

There was a buzzing sound coming from this tree. *What is that?* Rosco sniffed the tree. It smelled just like all the others. He looked up and saw something round sticking to one of the limbs. It had red things with wings flying around and crawling over it.

The buzz was the sound of their wings, and Rosco was fascinated by what they were doing. He sat down and barked at them. They ignored him. Rosco wanted to play.

"Rosco, get away from that tree," the master called.

Rosco looked at the master, then back at the tree. He knew the master was calling him away, but he wanted to have some fun.

"Rosco, those are red wasps you're messing with, and they'll sting you," he heard the master's warning.

Making up his mind, Rosco jumped, barking his invitation for his newfound friends to come and play with him.

He ran around the tree, but the flying red things just continued to ignore him. He jumped again, but this time he grabbed the limb from where the round thing was hanging. He sunk his teeth in and shook the limb. Now he had their attention!

The buzzing red demons descended on him in a swarm.

Rosco ran from the tree, yelping in pain. The wasps stung him on his ears, his legs, and his tail.

Rosco ran in circles and then rolled in the grass, but the swarm was still on him. Desperate, he headed for home and the safety of his porch.

Finally, the wasps stopped swarming him and returned to their tree. Rosco stood on the porch steps, crying and rubbing his swollen nose with his aching paws.

Soon the master came. "Sorry, boy, but I told you that red wasps are not to be messed with. You have to learn to listen to those who have more life experience," he said softly.

The master returned to the house with a gel that he rubbed on Rosco's nose, paws, and everywhere the wasps had stung him. Ms. Trudy came out and spoke to the master. "Ken, you should not have let him out of your sight. The little fellow does not know to leave wasps alone."

"He knows now," Ken said.

"Yes, and look at him. You promised me that you would take care of him. Now he's lying here covered in wasp stings, swollen, and crying out in pain. You ought to be ashamed of yourself, Ken Bangs."

"Hey, Sugar, I tried to call him off, but he just kept jumping on their tree. He even jumped up and grabbed the limb where they put their nest. They had pretty much ignored him until then. But once he did that, it was on like Donkey Kong," Ken said.

"It was an amazing thing to see. They swarmed him from head to tail and at every point in between. He was running in circles, rolling in the grass, and snapping at them. Then he hightailed it for the porch, and you should have seen that boy run. I tell you, Trudy, that little man can run!"

"Hush! You seem to be enjoying it. Did you stand there and watch, or did you try to help him?" Trudy asked.

"Help him? I couldn't get close, or I would have been stung, too," Ken said, shaking his head.

"I wish you had. Then maybe you would have more compassion for this poor little man," Trudy scolded.

Ken sighed, shook his head, and walked away.

Ms. Trudy had a bottle and a spoon in her hand. She poured something from the bottle into the spoon and said, "Here, Rosco, take this. It will ease the pain and take that swelling down some."

Rosco lapped the red liquid from the spoon and then lay down. Ms. Trudy rubbed him with a cold, wet towel until Rosco drifted off to sleep.

Ms. Trudy watched as Rosco twitched and whimpered. His legs jerked and he barked. She knew he was dreaming about his stinging introduction to red wasps.

And she was right. In his dreams, Rosco was running from an endless line of swarming red demons. There were so many that the very air seemed to have a red tinge. No matter which way he turned, the stinging menace found him.

Not one inch of his body was safe from the fiery thrusts of their stinging lances. He remembered one of the demons flying straight for the end of his nose. He had snapped his mouth closed on the winged buzzer only to experience pain in his tongue. No matter how hard he tried, he could not manage to spit the pain from his mouth. That had been the end for Rosco.

Conceding the battle, he had turned for home and his porch. In his dreams, he reached the porch, and the stinging stopped. But the dream would begin again. The dream recycled over and over, and with each playing, the lesson was ground deeper and deeper into his memory.

Never again would Rosco challenge the red wasp. Never again would he ignore the advice of those with more life experience. Rosco had learned.

## Rocket Man

Rosco woke early. His eyes were swollen almost closed, and he could barely see between the slits. His nose ached, and his paws were sore. His first thought was about the relief Ms. Trudy had brought him; he needed more. He had to find Ms. Trudy.

He trotted around to the front porch because he had learned Ms. Trudy came out this door as she began her morning walk. The door opened, but instead of Ms. Trudy, it was Ken coming out, and he was pulling a bag on wheels.

Rosco was confused. He sat and watched as the master opened Ms. Trudy's car door and put the bag in the back. Then the master returned to the house, came out with another bag, and put it into the car. Rosco felt uneasy about this.

Ah, here came Ms. Trudy. Rosco recognized her step. His tail was already thumping the porch when she came through the door.

"Well, good morning, my little man. Oh, just look at my baby. I know you must be hurting from all those stings. I believe they covered every inch of my little man's body. You are so swollen. I wish I could give you more medicine, but I don't think it would be safe for you. I am sorry, Rosco, but you have to suffer through this," she said.

Her voice was always so soft, so sweet. Somehow, it always made his tail wag even faster. She bent over to rub his ears. Rosco loved for Ms. Trudy to rub his ears. He loved it even now when they were sore from all the stings. Her hands were soft and smelled good, different from the master's.

"Rosco, I'm going to be gone awhile. But Ken will be here, and he'll take good care of you. I will pray for you every day and look forward to coming home to see you. Be a good boy, drink your milk, and grow up big and strong for me," Ms. Trudy said softly.

Rosco's tail was still wagging, but deep down in his heart, there was a dull pain. She was leaving. He didn't understand all the details, but he knew Ms. Trudy was going, and he did not like it.

He sat and watched as the master hugged Ms. Trudy, kissed her, and prayed for her. Then she got into the car and drove away.

The master sat on the steps, and Rosco could tell he was sad. Rosco leaned in against the master's side. The master's arms went around him and pressed Rosco to his chest.

A tear dropped onto Rosco's face, and he looked up to see the master's eyes overflowing. "She'll be okay, boy. She's going to Israel on a prayer ministry trip, and she'll be home in three weeks. It's a long time, but we'll make it," the master's voice was not as strong as usual.

"Come on now; we have lots to do. This farm will not work itself." The master sat Rosco down and walked to the barn. Rosco followed and watched as Ken climbed onto the tractor and headed out to the fields.

Rosco had seen this before. He knew the master would be on the tractor all day, mowing the pastures and working the garden. The sun was hot, and the steps just too many for Rosco to follow along. He gave up and walked back to his porch. His little head was low, his tail was down, and his spirit was heavy. *'Ms. Trudy, please come home,'* he wished silently.

Finally, Rosco heard the tractor motor stop. He headed for the barn. He knew that the workday was over and the master would be coming home. Ken walked out of the barn, saw Rosco, and called out to him. "Hey, Rosco. Come on boy. We're going to eat us a steak tonight."

*Steak! And steaks had bones.* Rosco ran in circles, jumping and barking in his excitement. He watched as the master opened the grill, fired it up, and brought out the steak.

He loved to hear the sizzle as the meat was dropped onto the hot grill. The smoke and the smell of cooking beef caused his mouth to water. No matter how hard he tried, Rosco could not stop licking his lips. Finally, the steak was ready.

Rosco jumped and begged as the master took the steak off the grill. He waited patiently as the master carried the food into the house. He knew the master would eat, and then he would bring Rosco some of the steak and the bone.

Rosco listened to the master's steps as he approached the door. There he was, and he was carrying the whole steak on a plate.

"I thought I would eat out here with you tonight, Rosco," he said. Rosco watched as the master carried his food to the table, pulled up a chair, and sat down.

Rosco leaped into the chair next to the master. He put his front paws on the table and watched as the master cut the steak. Rosco could see the plate was full of other food, but he kept his eyes on the steak.

Then the phone rang inside the house. "Oh, I bet that's Trudy," the master said as he ran inside.

Rosco looked at the door, which was now closed. He could hear the master talking inside the house. He looked at the steak. It smelled so good. He looked at the back door. It was still closed. He looked at the steak again, and before he could stop himself, he had it in his mouth and was down on the porch chewing as fast as he could.

Out of nowhere, Ginger and the other dogs appeared. They were suddenly gone, taking the steak and the bone with them.

Rosco jumped back up into the chair. He had seen the juice running out of the steak when the master had cut into it. It was still there on the plate! Rosco licked it up, savoring every drop. The taste of the meaty juice quickened his appetite. The juice had been mixed in with the beans. Rosco just kept licking, and soon the beans were all gone, too.

"*Rosco*! What are you doing? You ate my steak and my beans. I can't believe you ate all of that!" the master's voice told Rosco that he was not pleased.

Rosco was down on the floor and had rolled onto his back. That sometimes helped when the master was upset. He would lie there looking at the master, and gradually the master would relax and rub his belly. But it did not work this time.

The master picked up the now empty plate and walked back into the house. Rosco felt bad. He was sorry about the beans, but he was sorry that he was being blamed for eating the steak when it was Ginger and the posse who had taken it.

Rosco lay there thinking. *What would the master do?* Then his belly rumbled. Hey, what was that?

He rolled over onto his side and looked at his now swollen and protruding belly. Wow, it was pooched out. His belly was expanding even more, and there was more rumbling. The pressure was building up, more and more pressure.

Rosco stood, and the pressure was just overwhelming. He felt his belly rumble and then there was a loud noise coming out of his bottom. He scooted across the porch, and it seemed the sound was chasing him.

*What's this?* Rosco could feel the pressure building again, and it scared him. Off he went, running across the yard, trying his best to escape the noises in his belly and those that were blowing out of him and chasing him across the yard. Round and around in circles, he went until exhaustion pulled him down. He collapsed in the grass, panting.

"Let that be a lesson for you, Rosco," the master said. "Those beans are not good for puppies. They blow you up like the Goodyear blimp and send you scooting across the yard like a rocket man. I think I'll call you Rosco Beans, the Rocket Man," the master said.

Rosco did not know how to take what the master was saying. Was he angry? Rosco just sat looking at him. He noticed that the corners of the master's eyes were crinkling. Rosco didn't know why, but his tail started to wag, and then there was a smile on the master's face. He was laughing and bending over to rub Rosco's ears. "I am just kidding. You are Rosco Jack of Gateway Farm, and I love you. Come on, boy. Let's get you on the porch for the night. It looks like we have a storm coming," the master said, looking at the dark wall of clouds.

Rosco had felt the change. The air was becoming heavy, and there was a smell to it. He lifted his nose and sniffed. *Water. The air smelled like water.*

As Rosco sat considering this, a line of fire streaked across the sky, followed by an explosion of sound that sent Rosco jumping for his porch. He bounded up the steps and slid under one of the chairs as the sky opened and the rain came riding in on a wind that drove it under the chair where Rosco was huddled.

Scared and wet, Rosco dashed through the rain to the back door. He scratched and barked, hoping the master would hear.

The door opened, and there was the master with a warm towel, picking him up and rubbing him dry.

"It's all right, Rosco. That's just thunder. But this storm is going to last through the night, and you need a dry place to sleep, so I'm going to spread you a warm rug here in the laundry room. Sleep well, my little man," the master rubbed his head.

The master turned off the light and closed the door. Rosco lay down on the rug and was instantly asleep.

## Peace, The Promise of Prayer

Morning dawned bright and clear. The air, laden with the smell of rain the night before, was now fresh and clean. The master opened the laundry room door and smiled at Rosco.

"Good morning, my man. Sleep well, did you? Come out with me, while I feed the big dogs, and then we'll get your breakfast," the master said.

Walking out onto the porch, Rosco heard a new sound. It was coming from the pond. He ran down the steps to get a better look.

"Hey, boy," the master said. "Those are geese. They often overnight on the pond this time of year. It's safe to look them over, but don't get too close.

That mother goose will figure you to be a danger to her brood. You don't want her after you. She is twice your weight and will give you a flogging every bit as severe as the one you got from those wasps."

Rosco trotted over and sat down by the master's boot. As Rosco watched, the mother goose turned towards the bank and led her little ones out of the water. Something began to stir in Rosco. He didn't understand the emotion, but it felt so right.

The unknown force seemed to be pulling Rosco toward the pond and the geese. He stood and walked a few steps toward the pond. A low growl started in his chest.

Ginger and the other dogs looked at him as if to say, '*You don't want to do that, pup.*' Ginger walked over and lay down in front of Rosco, blocking his path. It was if she were telling him, '*Don't mess with that mother goose, or you'll be sorry.*'

Rosco paid no attention to Ken, Ginger, or the posse. He stepped around Ginger in a slow, stiff-legged stalk.

Ken stood aside and watched Rosco. Part of him wanted to reinforce the warnings just given, but he also wanted to see what would happen.

He was curious about Rosco. He had seen evidence of the pup's courage when he'd tackled Collins for peeing on him. Now Ken was beginning to suspect that there was a hunter buried deep within Rosco. Here he was exhibiting traits of the hunter without even realizing what he was doing.

Ken glanced toward the pond and saw the mother goose leading her little brood from the water. He knew the mother goose would defend her young with a ferocity that one had to see to appreciate. He wouldn't let it go too far, but this was another life lesson Rosco needed to learn.

With a low growl, Rosco dropped to his belly and began to crawl, inch by inch, toward the geese. His ears were pulled down flat on his head, his tail was pointed straight out, and he was focused squarely on the little flock.

The mother goose had seen Rosco start his stalk when he had stepped around Ginger. She stood watching him. When he dropped to the ground, she stretched her neck, lowered her head, and spread her wings. She called softly to her little ones, and they gathered behind her.

It was too much for Rosco. He was up and running without even thinking about it. His lips pulled back, his muscles tensed, and his senses were heightened by centuries of genetic programming. Rosco was on the hunt.

His mouth opened as he gathered himself for the launch that would land him squarely on target. As he made his leap, he became conscious of a white blur lifting off the ground to meet him in midair.

He was blasted from his daze by a fury of feathers beating him in the face. The counterattack turned him aside and sent him rolling through the grass. The white fury was all over him, pecking, flogging, and squawking.

Finally, able to get his feet under him, Rosco tried to run for home. Rosco, the hunter, was buried under the continuing onslaught of the mother goose. He could not escape her. A movement caught his eye, and he saw the master running to the battle, waving his arms and shouting. Suddenly, the feathered fury was gone.

Rosco turned in full flight towards the master, not slowing until he had found protection behind Ken's legs. There the pup sat, peeking around the master's boots at the flogging monster disguised as a mother goose.

Without meaning to, Rosco let a *woof* escape.

Instantly the wings went up, the neck stretched out, and an angry squawk invited him back for round two. Rosco declined with a whimper.

The mother goose squawked at him once again and then, in disdain, turned her back to him and gathered her goslings. The young ones cast a contemptuous look at Rosco and fell in line behind their mom. Off they went, back to the water, where they swam a lap around the pond in celebration of Mom's victory over the pup called Rosco.

Rosco felt the hot flush of shame and turned for his porch. The master followed without saying anything. His heart ached for Rosco, but he knew these things were necessary for Rosco to learn.

Rosco heard splashing, and looking to the pond; he saw Big Blue wallowing in the shallows. He seemed to be laughing at Rosco. Rosco imagined what the big fish was thinking, "*Hey, mighty dog! Want some more of mother goose? Boy, you are something. All those teeth and done in by flapping wings. Get back up on the porch and have the master, as you call him, bring you a bowl of milk!*"

Rosco dropped his head and whimpered. Gone was the primeval hunter, replaced by a thoroughly flogged puppy.

He trudged to the porch and hid behind Ms. Trudy's big ivy plant. A great sigh worked its way up and out of his chest.

He so wanted to be Rosco Jack of Gateway Farm. But the mother goose had just proved that, as of yet, he was only Rosco, the pup.

Rosco sulked around on the porch most of the morning. Ginger and her posse joined him as the boredom was about to overpower his shame and lead him into more trouble. Rosco watched as Ginger lifted her nose, sniffed the air, and walked to a sheltered corner at the back of the porch to lie down.

The other dogs soon followed suit. But Rosco was restless. He started towards the steps. Ginger growled at him. He stopped, glanced over his shoulder, and then looked back towards the steps. Ginger growled again. Her intent was clear. Rosco turned back and sat down.

Soon, Ginger was asleep. Rosco stood as quietly as possible. Ginger didn't move, but Gracie raised her head and looked at him, her eyes full of criticism. He hesitated, then decided to make a run for it. He padded softly forward and down the steps and took off. He was off the porch and running free.

Rosco saw the master driving his golf cart toward the pond. Great, he thought. The master had been saying that he was tired of that big blue fish and was going to fry him up. Rosco didn't know what that meant, but if it had anything to do with Big Blue getting his due, Rosco wanted to be there to see it firsthand.

After checking carefully, he was satisfied that the mother goose and her gang of eight had moved on. Rosco followed the master and joined him on the dock. Rosco remembered that the dock was built to extend over the pond, and he carefully approached the edge to orient himself and avoid another unplanned trip into the deep.

Rosco saw that the master had his grill with him, and he watched as the master carried it up onto the dock. The master started a fire in the grill and walked back to the Gator to get meat. Rosco's mouth was already watering.

The master put hamburger patties and hot dogs on the hot grill. Then, looking to the wall of clouds building in the north, he zipped his jacket, pulled his hat down a little tighter on his head, and then sat down in his webbed chair. Rosco watched as the master pulled a book from his jacket pocket and started to read.

Rosco was focused on the tantalizing smell coming from the smoking grill. He watched as the smoke drifted across the pond, and he thought about the coming feast.

Out of his peripheral vision, Rosco saw movement in the water. It started as a ripple. It moved around the edge of the pond, gaining speed and growing higher and higher until it was no longer a ripple but a wave. Rosco stood and leaned out over the water, looking down at an angle to see what was causing the surge.

There was Blue, and he was leading a long line of other fish. They were swimming abreast of each other to create as big a wave as possible. Rosco knew what was coming. He moved away from the edge of the dock and barked at the master. The master looked at Rosco and went back to reading.

Blue and his gilled friends had drawn even with the dock. In unison, each fish arched up and out of the water, nosed over, and turned in midair to land on their sides as they cannonballed back into the water. A wall of green pond water jetted up and over the dock, soaking the master and dousing the fire in the grill.

Rosco had never seen the master angry until now. He jumped out of his chair, sputtering and stomping around, yelling that this meant war. He declared that there could be no peace with that rogue fish and that it was time to bring things to a head.

Rosco heard splashing and looked out over the water toward a big stump at the far end of the pond. Blue had leaped out of the water and was perched on the stump, his band of jumpers splashing in celebration around the stump.

Rosco watched as the master turned redder and redder. Finally, the master pointed straight at Blue and said, "That tears it, Blue. I will not rest until I have you out of this big pond and into the little one. You won't be able to cause so much trouble over there. I tell you, Blue, you have gone too far this time."

Rosco looked from Ken to where Blue was holding court on the stump. As he watched, Blue slid off the stump and dived toward the deep part of the pond.

*'It seems almost as if Blue is mocking the master, as if he is saying that he is too smart to be caught and transferred to the little pond,'* Rosco thought.

The master pulled the grill off the deck, poured the water out of it, and loaded it onto the cart.

Rosco trotted alongside as the master drove slowly to the house. Rosco watched as the master took off his squishing boots, poured the water from them, and went inside without another word. Rosco had never seen him like this.

Rosco walked around the corner of the porch to his favorite sleeping mat and lay down. It had not been a good day for him or the master. It had been a real train wreck.

There was tension in the air. Things were building between the master and Blue. Rosco could feel it. There was a real blowup coming.

Then there was the matter of the big cat out there in the woods, and he sure hoped that mother goose and her brood of smirking goslings would hit the road soon.

If only Ms. Trudy were here. She would know what to say to make things better. Rosco knew the first thing she would do was pray. Ms. Trudy always said that *'peace was the promise of prayer.'*

Rosco didn't know how to pray, but he knew it worked. Ms. Trudy would lift her hands and start praying, and peace would flood in. She had promised that she would pray for them while she was away. Rosco sure hoped she remembered her promise.

## The Enemy in the Snow

Rosco noticed the wind increasing some as the day died. It was pushing a wall of clouds out of the north toward the back porch.

The air seemed to have a bluish tint, and Rosco found he was shivering. He now understood why Ginger had led the posse to the porch and had curled up in a protected corner. She had known the storm was coming and found her spot to ride it out.

Rosco trotted over to where the members of the posse were all bedded down. Wiggling his way in, he lay next to Ginger.

She raised her head to look at him and then moved slightly to allow him to lie against her side. Here the wind could not reach him, and he was able to draw heat from Ginger. Darkness fell, and Rosco experienced a blue norther for the first time.

The night winds swept across the farm, leaving a hoary frost that snapped through the air before settling on the grass. The other dogs seemed to bear up under the onslaught more easily than Rosco. They lay still, sleeping deeply, wrapped in their layers of thick fur.

But for Rosco, it was much different. He weighed a mere six pounds and was a shorthaired dog. He suffered without a blanket of long fur, shivering through the long hours of darkness. He slept little and realized for the first time how much his survival would rely on protection from the elements.

Morning dawned with metallic grey skies and a sharp north wind. Rosco and the posse remained huddled together until the door opened and the master stepped out to feed them breakfast. Rosco was hungry, and he bounded up and around the corner of the porch, only to bounce back as that north wind hit him.

The brutal cold turned him and sent him right back to his warm spot next to Ginger. She snorted her frustration with Rosco but allowed him to wiggle in closer.

The north wind kept blowing, and the temperatures continued to drop. Rosco peered over Ginger and saw that the air was filled with big, white flakes. There were so many of them that it was hard to see the pond. He turned his head towards the barn, but he could see nothing except wave after wave of blowing white flakes.

The snow fell through the afternoon and into the evening. As the darkness pushed the day aside, Rosco felt Ginger tense up. Suddenly, she stood with a growl. Instantly all the other dogs were on their feet and alert.

Rosco stood too, but he didn't know why. Then he heard the coyotes.

Their high-pitched yelping filled the night. They were throwing out a challenge for the right to possess and hunt the land. And it sounded as though they greatly outnumbered Ginger and the posse.

Ginger led the posse to the edge of the porch. Rosco followed. Ginger stopped, turned, and nudged him back with her nose. The other dogs waited patiently as she made it clear to Rosco that he could not go with them.

Then they were gone, into the woods, running to the fight. Rosco listened as the combatants came together. He trembled, not from fear but from a surge of adrenaline and the desire to be part of the battle.

It ended as suddenly as it had begun. Rosco could hear the coyotes as they cried out in surrender and fled the violence visited on them by Ginger and her crew. Victory!

Rosco ran around in circles. He jumped and barked out his elation. His ears perked up as he heard the familiar step of Ginger. He leaned forward and watched as the posse trotted out of the forest.

Ginger, Bo, Gracie, Mercie, and Collins were all there. They trotted forward with heads held high, flush with the glory of having met and defeated the enemy.

Rosco's heart swelled with pride. But when, oh when, would he get to be a full member of the Gateway Posse? When could he go to battle with the best?

## The Power of Love

Morning came, and the snow stopped. Rosco blinked at the dazzling display of sunbeams bouncing off the frosty blanket that covered Gateway. He followed as Ginger led her posse off the porch and down to the pond.

The big dogs trotted along with no problems, but Rosco found that his legs were too short for the deep snow. He turned back, crying every step of the way.

'*Why do I have to be so little? Collins is two months older than me and is already running with the big dogs. He had even fought with them last night.*' Rosco knew he was a puppy, but he wondered if he would ever grow big enough to run with the posse.

Rosco trudged up the steps and lay down. He heard the master coming and saw that Ginger was with him. She climbed up the steps, nudged him with her nose, and then licked his face. She lay down beside him and looked up at the master as he began to speak.

"Listen, Rosco. I want you to understand something. Some dogs are big, some are little, but they are all dogs.

It's not the size that makes the difference. It's the commitment to paying the price to be the best that you can be," he paused and looked out across the snowy pastures.

Then he continued, "I saw what happened when the posse went out after those coyotes. Ginger didn't let you go with them, not because of your size, but because she has not had the time to teach you yet.

You have to trust her and wait. She will bring you into the posse when the time is right and teach you how to protect this land and our family. You have to learn self-discipline, and you must not quit when the going gets rough. Is that a deal?"

Rosco didn't understand all that the master was saying, but he sensed that the master and Ginger were taking care of him. Ginger leaned over and licked his face, and the master laughed. "See, Ginger, agrees with me. She knows best; you listen to her," he said, rubbing Rosco's ears again.

Rosco's day had grown better. In the midst of his celebration, he saw Ginger's ears go up. In a flash, she was off the porch and running for the front gate. Rosco was right behind her. He saw Ginger start jumping and barking.

Then Rosco saw the white car coming through the gate. *Ms. Trudy is home!*

He ran and jumped, rolled in the snow, and sat as the car stopped. The window rolled down, and there was her face. Ms. Trudy was saying hello to Ginger, and then she turned to look at Rosco.

"Well, hello, my little man. Aren't you so pretty? I do believe you have grown.? Come to the house so I can pet all my babies," there was a smile in her voice.

Rosco and Ginger followed along as Ms. Trudy drove to the house. Ken was coming down the front steps, holding his arms wide to greet Ms. Trudy. They embraced, and Ken gave thanks to the Lord for bringing his beloved home safely.

Then she turned to the dogs. She patted and spoke lovingly to each one. And then it was Rosco's turn. She picked him up and held him to her chest. He licked her face and nuzzled in with his head under her chin. Rosco's heart was experiencing life's greatest gift: to love and be loved. What a wonderful day! Ms. Trudy was home.

Ken carried Ms. Trudy's bags into the house. Trudy still held Rosco and carried him up onto the porch.

"Ken," she called. "Will you bring me that red bag with Rosco's name on it?"

Ken walked out of the house and handed Trudy the bag. She sat Rosco on his pillow and gave him a rawhide bone. Rosco smelled it, licked it, and then lay down and started to chew.

The more he chewed, the better it got. Soon Rosco was focused solely on the bone, and Ms. Trudy left him to his chewing and walked into the house.

"That boy is chewing away," she said to Ken. "He'll get hours of enjoyment out of that little chew bone."

"Don't count on it," Ken said. "His puppy teeth have dropped out, and his permanent ones are in. He'll chew that thing up in no time."

Later, Rosco lay on the porch, his new bone all chewed up and gone. He was aware of the changing of the seasons. He had arrived in the heat of the summer when even the nights were uncomfortably warm. But now, the days were mild, and the nights were downright nippy.

Rosco had also noticed that the trees were changing. The leaves were curling up and falling. Ken and Roy, the Forman of Gateway Farm, were not mowing as often, and it seemed to rain more.

Rosco noticed that Ms. Trudy and Ken were bustling about in the house a lot. He couldn't identify the cause for it, but something was happening. He could feel the excitement.

Then one morning, while Ken was feeding breakfast to the posse, Ms. Trudy stepped out onto the porch and pointed to the sky.

"It looks like that storm the weatherman forecast is building there in the north. If you want to get a turkey today, might be your last chance for a while," she said.

Rosco watched Ken turn and look to where Ms. Trudy had pointed. "Yep, believe you're right, Sugar. Let me feed the posse, and I'll get my gun and go see what I can do," Ken replied.

Ken walked up the steps and into the house as the posse finished the last of the breakfast. The dogs had begun to trot away when the door opened, and Ken came out, carrying his shotgun and wearing his hunting hat and vest.

Now excitement filled the air, and Rosco knew exactly why. They were going to the forest with Ken. He had seen this before, but Ken and Ginger always made him stay behind. This time he was going. To be sure, Rosco took off running for the trail Ken always used when entering the forest.

He heard Ken laugh. Ms. Trudy called out, "Ken, don't take Rosco. He's too little yet, and I couldn't stand it if he got hurt."

"We have to cut those apron strings sometime, Sugar. Now seems as good a time as any. I'll watch him, and he'll be all right," Ken said.

Rosco ran on. He was on the hunt. He looked around, hoping that the mother goose was not out today.

Ken called to Rosco, "Come here, boy. Get back here. You'll scare everything in the woods away, tromping around like that. Maybe Trudy was right. Maybe I should have left you home."

Rosco stopped and sat. Ginger trotted up, sniffed him, and nuzzled him with her warm nose as if to say, *'It's okay. We've all have to learn.'*

She trotted forward, and the posse fanned out around her. Rosco watched as they crept stealthily through the forest. Each dog had their nose in the air. Rosco knew they were testing for a scent, but which one?

Ginger suddenly dropped to her belly, and the posse followed suit. They lay perfectly still, ears perked forward, concentrating on one spot behind a big bush in front of Ginger.

Ken crouched on one knee and raised the shotgun to his shoulder. Rosco didn't know what to do. He was trembling from the tension, and without meaning to, he barked.

While the bark was still in his throat, Rosco heard a roar as the biggest bird he had ever seen exploded from the ground with wings beating the air as it struggled for altitude.

Rosco saw a blur of bluish-green and grey topped with a long red beard as the bird folded its legs out of sight into its' belly feathers.

Rosco looked at Ken. Ken lowered the gun and smiled as the majestic bird banked left and disappeared behind a giant pine.

"Wow," Ken said. "Have you ever in your life witnessed such beauty and power? No way I could kill such a magnificent bird. We'll eat on Thanksgiving Day, and when we do, I will remember this and thank the Lord for allowing me to witness His creation. Come on, boys and girls. Let's go home. What do you say?" Ken laughed.

It was fine with Rosco. That turkey hadn't done him any harm. Live and let live was his motto; a creed that would be brought back to him soon.

Ms. Trudy was gone when they came home from the turkey hunt. Rosco followed Ken into the house and saw him pick up a note she had left. He heard Ken laugh and say, "Listen to this, Rosco.

Dear Ken, I have gone to the grocery store to buy food for the Thanksgiving meal. And yes, I will be buying a turkey because I know my man, and I know that you can no more kill one of those beautiful creatures than you could shoot Rosco."

Ken continued to read, and Rosco heard him say, "Heard from the kids, and they will all be here around noon tomorrow. Be back soon. Would you please give Rosco a bath so he will be fresh and clean for tomorrow? Love you, Trudy.'"

Ken said, "Our family is coming, and they will love you! Miranda will have you sitting at a desk with bows in your hair while she teaches school. And K.W. will be showing you how to play video games. I love this time of year, getting to be with family."

He looked around for Rosco, but Rosco was not to be found. Rosco had heard the word "bath" and had run to his hiding place under Ms. Trudy's chair.

Ken laughed and said, "Come on out of there, big boy. It's a little cool to give you a bath. If you'll stand still and let me brush you down good and sprinkle some of that baby powder that Trudy likes on you, maybe we can get by without having to get you and me all wet."

*'That is the best deal I have heard today,'* thought Rosco as he crawled out from under the chair.

Sure enough, the storm hit not long after Ms. Trudy came home. The wind slammed against the house as it whistled past on its way south. Ken pulled on his coat and hat and walked to the barn to make sure the posse was bedded down and protected from the wind.

Rosco curled up on his rug next to Ms. Trudy. He didn't mind waiting for better weather to join the posse.

The morning came with grey skies and freezing rain. The pellets pinged against the windows, and the wind shook the house. But it was snug inside.

Ms. Trudy was cooking, and the house was filled with the smell of a feast. It was almost more than Rosco could stand. He drooled and licked his lips so much that Ken laughed and told Ms. Trudy to get him a bib.

Just before noon, Rosco heard a car horn. It was the family. Rosco sat and watched as they all rushed inside out of the weather. After all the hugging and kissing, Ken said, "Hey, I want you all to meet the newest member of this family. His name is Rosco Jack, and he came to us as a castaway."

All eyes turned toward him. Each one took turns kneeling and rubbing his head. First was Miranda, then a woman named Kristen, who reminded Rosco of Ms. Trudy. He could see the love on her face.

Then there was Anel. She had the gentlest eyes, and Rosco felt her love. Next was a boy who called the master Papa.

Rosco noticed that he stood straight as an arrow and had a slight smile on his lips. Standing next to K.W. was a man that the master called Son, and Anel called Ken.

Rosco sniffed this Ken, and then he sniffed K.W. They smelled like the master. Rosco looked at them again; they looked like the master too.

Rosco watched as the family laughed and joked with each other. He saw how they seemed to each prefer the other, how gentle and kind they were when speaking one to the other. But the greatest witness was that of the love that flowed from them. On top of that, they did not see him as a runt who had been cast away. They all accepted him for who he was.

Rosco was overcome with all the attention. He was so excited he made a puddle on Ms. Trudy's favorite rug, and she was not happy.

But Miranda said, "It's okay, Nonnie. Sometimes my dog Moose has accidents, and I know how to clean them up."

While Miranda was cleaning up the puddle, Ms. Trudy, Kristen, and Anel were putting the food on the table. Then it was time to eat.

K.W. pulled an extra chair up next to him and patted it for Rosco. The pup did not need a second invitation and bounded into the chair. He stood on his back legs and put his front paws on the table. He looked around and licked his lips.

"Oh, no you don't, Rosco. Dogs are not allowed at my Thanksgiving table. You get down right this second," Ms. Trudy said sternly.

Rosco slunk out of the chair and sat looking at K.W.

"Nonnie, let him sit here. He won't hurt anything, and Papa said he was the family's newest member. The family gets to sit at the table, right?" K.W. asked.

"K.W. has got you there, Nonnie," Papa laughed.

Rosco looked at Ms. Trudy. Ms. Trudy was looking at the long faces of Miranda and K.W.

Finally, she said, "Oh, what's the harm? Okay, Rosco. You're in the house, so I guess you might as well have a seat at the table."

In a flash, Rosco was in the chair looking at the bird that Ms. Trudy had brought home and cooked. This one did not look anything like the one they had seen in the forest, and it smelled a whole lot better.

Ken, the master, said grace and the family began to fill their plates. When everyone had a full plate, Miranda said, "What about Rosco?"

Ken laughed and left the table to return with an aluminum foil plate, which he placed in front of Rosco. He then pulled one of the wings from the turkey, stripped the meat from the bone, and put the meat on the plate. Rosco ate it before Ken could sit back down in his chair.

The family laughed, and Rosco got a second helping.

It was the best day of Rosco's life. The house was full of love. Something stirred in the core of his being, and he resolved that this was his family and he would protect them from all harm. His size did not matter. This was an issue of the heart. Rosco had learned the power of love and to be thankful for family.

## Rosco and the Pirate

Thanksgiving was over, and the family had gone home. The hustle and bustle of the holiday were done, and stillness had settled over the farm.

Rosco missed having all his family together. He especially missed Miranda and K.W.

He had run alongside them as they rode their bikes, had played fetch the stick, and had even allowed Miranda to put bows on his head. Gateway was not the same without them.

In the midst of his reverie, Collins walked over and lay down beside him. Rosco could tell he was restless. In a few minutes, Collins was up and trotting toward the woods. He stopped and looked back at Rosco.

Rosco lay still. Ginger never allowed any of the posse to go into the woods alone. He also knew that Collins loved to run the woods, chasing squirrels, rabbits and the occasional deer. He had seen him come back with his coat covered in mud and filled with burs.

Rosco knew that Collins considered himself to be slick. But he also knew it was only a matter of time until Ginger caught him sneaking off, and then it would not be pretty.

Still, for some reason, Rosco felt his curiosity stirring. *'What would it be like to sneak off and run with a big dog like Collins, just this one time,'* he found himself wondering.

Suddenly he was up and running for the woods with Collins. They splashed through the creek and lay down under a big Red Oak to catch their breath.

As they lay there, Rosco lifted his nose and sniffed. The air was full of wonderful scents. He smelled the musty leaves piled deep around the trees and then there was the smell of animals.

He sniffed again and was able to identify the scent of squirrels, rabbits, and even a snake. As he lay there daydreaming, he felt the atmosphere change. He looked at Collins, and saw that the big dog was focused on a tree in front of where they lay.

He turned to look at the tree and saw a giant squirrel. It was one of the big red ones that dwarfed the grey ones and ruled the forest.

The squirrel seemed not to have noticed them. He ran down the tree and sat at the base of it eating an acorn.

Finishing that one, he moved away from the tree and grabbed another one. Rosco glanced at Collins and saw him lick his lips. *'What? Is he drooling? Does he intend to eat that squirrel? Why would he want to do that, the master feeds us twice a day.'* Rosco was trying to figure out what Collins was thinking.

It didn't make sense to Rosco, but then Collins had a reputation for doing crazy stuff. Rosco didn't mind chasing a squirrel just for fun, but he didn't want to eat one.

He thought about it a little longer. The longer he thought about it, the more it seemed to be the thing to do. *'I am a dog, after all, and dogs eat squirrels, don't they?'* he asked himself.

As they lay there watching the squirrel eat acorns, Rosco took the opportunity to study Collins closely. He was a big dog, clumsy and different-looking. He was solid white.

And his eyes were strange. One was blue, and one was black, and each was surrounded by pink. Rosco had heard Ken's mom, Miss Flo, say, "I can't stand to look that dog in the face. He is wonk-eyed."

Rosco agreed, but he also knew that the pirate was a full-fledged member of the posse. Rosco was so busy looking at Collins that he unconsciously inched forward in the mass of fallen leaves, causing a terrible racket.

Collins looked around, and Rosco could see he was irritated.

*"Watch where you're going. Some hunter you are!"* his eyes seemed to shout at Rosco.

Collins looked back to where the squirrel had been, and Rosco looked too. The squirrel was gone. Collins snorted and stood, turning his back to Rosco as he trotted off to find another squirrel.

Rosco took the rebuke and followed. He was determined to stalk the woods in silence. He was going to eat a squirrel before this day was through.

Collins stopped after a while and lay down. Rosco looked around at all the acorns on the ground. There was some low brush just in front of them, and it provided cover, hiding them from all but the wariest eyes. This was a perfect spot to ambush a squirrel. Maybe they would get another big red one, and Collins would no longer be angry with him.

They lay still and quiet on the forest floor. Rosco was able to identify most of the sounds and smells of the forest. Here again, he caught the scent of rabbits, squirrels, birds, and snakes that lived here among the fallen timber and deep piles of leaves.

Then his nose found the smell of a big cat. Rosco could tell it was an old scent, one left when the cat had passed through, but it was a big cat just the same like the one that had taken his sister on that night so long ago. The memory sent a cold shiver of fear through Rosco.

Rosco heard Collins growl softly. He looked slowly to his left, and there it was, another red squirrel. This one was even bigger than the first one. The squirrel was coming down from a tree. He stopped halfway down and looked around carefully.

*'Surely he can see us,'* Rosco thought. But down he came. The squirrel sat at the base of the tree and twitched his bushy tail. Then, he was off and running.

The squirrel ran in a straight line from his tree to a spot beyond where Collins and Rosco lay hidden. Rosco could see the squirrel stuffing his mouth with acorns. Soon his cheeks were so full they looked deformed.

Without warning, Collins launched himself at the squirrel. Rosco was right behind him.

The squirrel spat the acorns and jumped sideways. Collins stretched his neck, opened his mouth and snapped his jaws closed on empty air. To add insult to injury, he landed hard, belly first, on the log from which the squirrel had launched his escape.

The squirrel had avoided Collins, but Rosco, who was right behind, caught him by the tail, in midair. Elation filled Rosco as he clamped his mouth closed on the squirrel's tail.

Pain filled Rosco's face as the squirrel turned and bit down on his lips, raked razor-sharp claws down each side of the pup's nose, and notched his ear with teeth like scissors as he climbed up Rosco's face and over his head.

Then he was gone. After running halfway up the nearest tree, the squirrel stopped and chattered a rebuke at the would-be hunters.

Collins was still recovering from having his breath knocked out when he'd belly flopped, and Rosco was writhing in pain, rubbing his face and head through the piled-up leaves. The squirrel ran up his tree, disappearing into the thick foliage at the top.

Rosco looked at Collins. Collins stood, shook himself and turned toward home.

On the way, they had to cross a small creek. It was running full from the recent snow that was now melting. Rosco stopped and looked at his reflection. Oh, no. His heart sank.

What he saw looking back at him was a tiny black dog with white spots, or was he white with black spots? Either way, the chewed lips, the scratched nose, and the notched ear were what stood out.

*'Will Ginger know what happened? Maybe she will think I got tangled up the barb wire fence again,'* he was thinking. Then he sighed and turned toward home. *'The truth always comes out. The best thing to do is just let the facts speak for themselves, and the facts are that I look exactly like a dog that has lost a fight with an angry red squirrel,'* he had already accepted his fate.

Collins continued toward home as Rosco examined himself in the stream. He was sitting in the clearing surrounded by the posse when Rosco came out of the woods. Ginger stopped sniffing Collins and turned to look at Rosco.

Her eyes were full of disappointment, *"Really, Rosco,"* they seemed to say.

He lowered his little head and stood still. His tail wagged slowly. The posse gathered around and sniffed him. Gracie licked his bleeding nose and then sat down as Ginger came over to where he stood.

She sniffed Rosco and then looked at his wounds. She growled her frustration at him as she smelled the squirrel and deep woods on him.

She turned to Collins. Her frustration was building as she thought about how he had led the puppy into such danger. She knew it could have been so much worse. What if they had run into a pack of coyotes or a bunch of wild hogs? She trembled at the possibilities.

Collins stared back at her as if to say, *"Ah, you think you know it all. You're just old and set in your ways. I'm a pirate. I do things my way, see?"*

The smirk on his face pushed her over the edge. With one leap, Ginger was on Collins.

She hit him chest high, knocking him onto his back. She stood over him with her lips pulled back, showing all her teeth. The growl coming from her throat left no doubt about her willingness to use them.

Collins did the smart thing for once. He lay back in submission.

Rosco watched this and knew that he had made a colossal mistake. From watching the posse, he knew they did things together for a reason. *'The forest is dangerous, and we go there together or not at all. And we do not kill for the sport of it. We kill to protect the farm, our people, or ourselves. We hunt, but always together and only when hungry. From now on, I will abide by these principles,'* he decided.

Collins whimpered out his submission. Ginger let him up and turned to Rosco.

He immediately lay down and rolled onto his back. Ginger stood over him for a minute to stress that she was dominant and that if he wanted to be a member of the posse, he had to follow her without question.

She nuzzled Rosco, and he stood. She was not ready to release him yet and lifted her lip in a snarl. Rosco slunk back down and put his head between his paws.

He knew she was driving home the lesson, and he stayed still, thinking, *'I am going to stop trying to be something that I am not. I am still a puppy, not a grown dog. I will accept that and allow myself time to grow and learn. I will use this time to prepare for adulthood. I will accept that I am small in stature. That is the way it is, and I will not fret over what I cannot change.*

*Instead, I will make the most of what I am. Ms. Trudy told me that the Lord made me with a plan and a purpose. She said He does not make junk, nor does He make mistakes. She said for me to find my purpose and that He would show me His plan.'*

Ginger seemed to sense that Rosco had made his decision and stepped back, allowing him to get up. She licked his face as if to say, *'This is over, but don't let it happen again.'*

Rosco spent the rest of the afternoon licking his wounds and thinking about what he had learned. He knew Ginger would teach him how to hunt, defend his people and his land, and navigate the dangers of Gateway Farm and the two thousand acres of forest that surrounded it. He decided that he was going to follow her and not Collins.

Collins left the porch as soon as they had finished eating the evening meal. Rosco followed him down the steps to see what he was up to.

Collins trotted to the pond, and Rosco went after him. Collins turned and headed for the front gate when they were out of sight of the house. Rosco knew that he had decided to leave Gateway Farm and the posse. He sat and watched Collins go.

Collins realized that Rosco was not following and stopped to look back. He wagged his tail in an invitation, but Rosco sat still. He looked at Collins, thinking, *'Don't do this. It is a mistake. You have everything here, and you are a member of the posse. All you have to do is follow the rules. But he knew that Collins could not follow the rules. It was as if the master had set his course when he named him The Pirate. Collins had to go his own way and learn his lessons,'* Rosco sighed and turned toward the dock. He glanced over his shoulder and saw Collins trot through the open gate.

Rosco remembered that Collins liked to visit a house down the road. The couple that lived there did not have any kids or pets. They were always really excited to see Collins, and he would sometimes spend the night over there. Rosco figured that would be his first stop. But odds were that Collins wouldn't stay there long; he wanted to be the captain of his fate and roam.

Rosco walked onto the dock and lay down. The sun was setting, and its' reflection in the water was beautiful. The quiet beauty gave him peace. He knew that Collins was making a mistake. Maybe Collins would realize that this place of peace was worth all the rules and return here someday.

## The Stump Too Far

Big Blue had been swimming, slowing around the big stump at the far end of the pond, when he saw Collins and Rosco approaching. He was hoping that the little one would jump into the water so he could have his revenge on the posse.

Blue hung around the stump for a minute until he realized that they were not there to swim. He sensed the tension in the air and swam over and lay under the dock watching.

He saw the one that Ken called The Pirate nuzzle around on the little one and then move off toward the front gate. He saw him stop and wag his tail as if asking Rosco to come with him. Blue waited to see what Rosco would do, then swam back a little from the dock to get a better look at the Pirate. That's when he knew that Collins was leaving the farm.

*'YES,'* he thought. *'One of the posse is leaving, and from the looks of him, he was going to grow into the biggest one of the bunch. Go on, Rosco, go with him,'* Blue was cheering Collins on in his mind.

Blue held his breath, waiting, and then Rosco laid down on the dock. *'Shoot,'* Blue thought.

He watched as Collins moved toward the gate and then swam back in to get a closer look at Rosco. As Blue got closer, he could see the scratches and cuts on Rosco's nose and ears. Then he smelled the squirrel on Rosco. *'It looks like little man tangled with a squirrel and lost. Just like mother goose, the big red squirrel sent him home a whimpering pup,'* Blue smiled at the thought.

Then, Blue heard a familiar sound, the sound of a squirrel chattering. He glanced over his shoulder and saw a fat grey squirrel searching the bank under the pecan tree. '*He is hungry and looking for his supper. Maybe I can use this to teach Rosco that I rule these waters. Maybe I can strike enough fear in him that he will not be jumping in and stirring up a mess in our home,'* Blue was hatching a plan in his mind.

Blue flipped his tail and shot across the pond to the bank where the pecan tree hung out over the water. Rosco heard the splash and turned to watch as Blue searched the shallows under the big pecan tree. Blue kept working until he was able to get a fallen pecan out of the shallows and into the deeper water.

Blue took the pecan in his mouth and swam to a stump that was about five yards out from the bank. He pushed himself up and out of the water just enough to place the pecan on top of the stump. Then he swam to a spot about halfway between the stump and the bank. He turned and winked at Rosco and slowly sank out of sight.

It wasn't long before the squirrel spotted the nut resting on the stump. Rosco could tell the squirrel wanted the pecan, but there was a lot of water between him and his prize. That presented a problem.

Rosco could tell the squirrel was thinking. He watched as the squirrel walked up and down the bank, put one paw forward to test the water, and then sat down to think some more.

Rosco could tell that the squirrel had decided to jump for the stump to get that pecan.

The squirrel ran back about six feet from the water's edge. He sat looking, and Rosco knew he was gauging the distance. He watched as the squirrel twitched his tail, gathered himself into a tight ball, and sprang forward, running as fast as he could. At the perfect spot, the squirrel launched into the air and sailed across the water to land on the stump.

Rosco yelped, excited that the squirrel had made it and was now busily devouring Blue's pecan. Then Rosco saw the trap that Blue had set. The squirrel realized it at the same time.

He had been able to run and leap across the water to land safely on the stump. Now, he was trapped on top of the stump with no opportunity to gain the momentum to return safely. The stump was too far from the bank.

The squirrel sat twitching his tail. He circled the stump, but nothing changed. Rosco could see the squirrel accept that he was going to get wet. He bunched himself into a tight little ball and exploded off the stump, stretching his body toward the safety of dry land.

He made it about halfway. As the squirrel dropped toward the water, Blue opened his mouth and swallowed him whole.

Rosco couldn't believe it. As he sat pondering what he had witnessed, he saw Blue surface under that same pecan tree. He watched as Blue gathered another pecan and swam back to the stump. Blue eased up out of the water, placed the nut in the exact middle of the stump, and turned and nodded at Rosco.

Blue swam to his halfway spot and slowly sank beneath the surface. It wasn't long before another squirrel spied the pecan. Rosco couldn't bear to watch it again. He turned and trotted toward the house.

As he went, he heard a gurgling sound. He paused and looked back. Blue was leaning against the stump, looking at him. Rosco could read his mind, *'Hey, where are you going? Don't have the stomach for watching a real hunter at work? Go on. Hang out with the dogs. Only the smartest and strongest can survive in these waters, and I am the strongest,'* Blue was smirking.

Rosco couldn't bear to look at Blue any longer. He hated how Blue had laid the trap for the squirrel, and he resolved to live and let live. He had also learned two other things.

First, look long and consider carefully before you leap. Second, overextending yourself limits your ability to manage your destiny.▯

## Night Visitors

Summer had passed, and now fall was quickly becoming winter. The nights were getting longer and colder. It rained nearly every day.

The rain began to fall one Sunday afternoon in December and continued day and night through Wednesday. Rosco was starting to worry.

The water was collecting across the yard and around the porch. His brief ventures off the porch for his personal needs left him soaked to the bone. He was chilled and had developed a cough.

Ms. Trudy came out to check on him and noticed the cough. "Ken, come out here, please."

Rosco heard Ken's steps as he walked through the house. The door opened, and the back floodlight came on.

"What is it, Dolly?" Rosco had noticed that Ken often called Ms. Trudy his dolly.

"Rosco is wet, and look, and he's shivering," Ms. Trudy said.

"Well, all right. I'll get a couple of towels and a dry blanket for him," the master replied.

"No, he has a cough too, and I want him inside and out of this weather," Ms. Trudy said as she picked Rosco up and cradled him to her chest.

"Now, Dolly, you know we can't take a wet, smelly dog inside the house. He belongs out here on the porch. I'll dry him off, and he'll do just fine," the master said.

"No, I want this little man inside where he will be warm. Look at him! He's as wet as a drowned rat," Ms. Trudy said, looking at the master.

"I give up," Ken said. "Come on, Rosco. You are making history here at Gateway Farm. We have never let a wet dog inside before."

Rosco remembered that Ken had let him into the laundry room during a big storm while Ms. Trudy was gone.

Ken opened the door. Rosco slipped in and sat quietly while Ms. Trudy heated a towel in the dryer. She wrapped him in it and talked sweetly as she dried him.

"Ken, bring Rosco a bowl of warm milk," she called out to the master.

"Now, Sugar, you are going to spoil him. He is a dog, and I don't want him getting used to all this pampering," the master answered.

"It's not pampering to give a sick puppy warm milk, and besides that, Rosco does NOT stink," Ms. Trudy said with a glance at the master.

"Right," Ken sighed. "He can stay in the laundry room, but that's where I'm drawing the line."

Ken walked into the kitchen, and Rosco heard the sounds that told him Ken was pouring a bowl of milk and putting it in the microwave.

Ken set the milk down. Rosco waited until Ken had walked out and closed the door.

Then he lapped up the warm milk, turned around a couple of times on the blanket and lay down. The blanket smelled like Ms. Trudy. It was so soft and dry. That, combined with his belly full of warm milk, put Rosco to sleep.

Seemed like he had just drifted off when he heard a strange noise outside. He listened as it came closer and closer to the porch. Then something scraped against the porch. Rosco sat up, fully alert.

He smelled something, something fishy. And there was a slithering, rasping sound, like something dragging across the porch. The noise stopped at the back door.

There was a pounding on the door. Rosco barked. He heard Ken get out of bed and saw light under the door leading into the kitchen.

Ken was coming. The door to the laundry room opened, and there stood Ken with a pistol in his hand. Rosco immediately covered his ears with his paws. He had seen Ken with this pistol at the pond shooting at Blue's squirrel stump. Rosco's ears had rung for three days afterward. He did not want to hear that again.

"What is that noise boy?" Ken whispered looking at Rosco.

The slithering sound came again, and Rosco felt the fur on the back of his neck stand up. He lowered his head toward the door and sniffed. There it was, that wet fishy smell again. Then it hit him; that was a fish on the porch. It was Big Blue.

Rosco looked up at the master and growled a warning. He saw Ken step toward the door and reach for the knob. Ken yanked the door open and stepped onto the porch.

Rosco winced as he heard Ken say, "Blue? What are you doing out at this hour, and how did you get from the pond to here?"

Rosco peeked around the doorjamb and saw Blue leaning against the porch rail. Rosco had never seen anything like it. Blue was wearing a yellow plaid raincoat. He didn't have any arms to put in the sleeves, so the coat was held in place by a clasp made out of an old fishhook, with a length of fishing line strung across his chest and tied to a button-hole.

A black slouch hat sat on the back of his head. He had a monocle on his right eye and a dried reed stuck under one fin, letting it serve as his cane.

Rosco leaned further out the door and saw a boat tied to the steps. A big bass sat at the oars, patiently waiting in the pounding rain.

Rosco saw the dismay on Ken's face and then looked at Blue. Blue had his gaze fixed on the pistol in Ken's hand, and Rosco knew he, too, was remembering the violence that could erupt from the barrel.

Blue tore his gaze away from the pistol and glared at the master. Rosco could read his thoughts, *"Hey, no need for firearms. And a little courtesy would be appreciated."*

Rosco was amazed at the gall of the big fish. He had left the pond and used the flood to make his way to the back porch. Why? Then he saw Blue flounce over to lean against the wall under the bright spotlight the master had left on when retiring for the night.

Blue made sure Ken was watching, then looked up at the light and wagged his head back and forth as if to say, 'Turn *that light off.'*

*'Are you kidding me? He is complaining about the light shining through the darkness and onto the pond waters,'* Rosco thought.

Rosco looked at his master. He watched as Ken looked from Blue to the light and then toward the pond. He saw when Ken realized what Blue was complaining about, and he saw the master's neck turn dark red as the blood began to rise in his anger.

"You dare wake me in the middle of the night to complain about *my* light shining across *my* farm and into *my* pond?" the master's voice was thick with emotion.

"Blue, I know that you all sleep under the dock and that floodlight cannot possibly shine there from here. But it doesn't make any difference if it does. I am the master of this farm, and you are but another fish in the pond. Get that in your head Blue or suffer the consequences," Ken fumed.

Blue edged away from the angry man a bit, and Ken looked toward the boat tied to the stairs. Rosco followed his look and saw scrawled in mud on the side of the boat, *'Gateway Pond Association,'* Then below that was another message in mud, *'Big Blue, President.'*

"Gateway Pond Citizens Association! Big Blue President! That's *my* boat! Blue, what are you doing with *my* boat?" Ken was sputtering.

The sound of a snort came from the boat, and Rosco looked that way.

The bass was looking at Ken with disdain, and Rosco could imagine his thoughts, '*Well hey, what with us being here on official Gateway Pond Association business and seeing as how we are aquatic animals and all, we naturally chose a boat as our mode of transport. Yours was the only one available, so we requisitioned it. Besides that, it is time you share the wealth with the folks. Share and share alike is our motto.*'

Rosco could see that the master did not like that. Ken's face was contorted and red. "Who's that you got rowing you around in my boat, Blue? Is that Billy, the bass that I have caught and released several times?

Maybe the next time, I won't be so compassionate. Maybe I won't practice catch and release anymore. Maybe I will throw what I catch on the bank for the night animals to feast on," Ken said, looking at the big bass.

Rosco glanced from Ken to Big Blue and then at Billy. A sudden gust of wind pushed the back of the boat around so that Billy was now next to the porch rail and within a few inches of where Ken stood holding his pistol. Billy was staring at Ken and slowly dropped his eyes to the pistol in Ken's hand.

Billy now had the floor. All eyes were on him. He looked at the pistol, then turned to look at the pond. He turned back to be sure Ken was looking at him and then slipped from the boat's seat into the bottom of the boat. A good amount of rainwater had collected there. Rosco saw Billy fill his mouth with the water and then turned and spit it toward Ken's pistol. The brackish stream of water flooded over the pistol and soaked Ken's hand and his pants.

Ken gasped. His lips moved, but no words came out.

Big Blue started to slither backward. He was flapping his fins at Billy as if to say, *'That's enough, Billy. It's okay, Mr. Ken. You go on back to bed, and we'll talk about all this at another time.'*

But Rosco could see it was too little, too late.

There was a hissing sound coming from between Ken's teeth. Rosco thought it sounded a lot like Ms. Trudy's teapot when she'd made tea for Ms. Cheryl and Ms. Charlotte.

Ken laid his pistol down and stepped forward onto the porch. He grabbed the large, long-handled net he kept hanging on the wall. It was designed to allow Ken to reach out and capture fish that he had hooked with his rod and reel.

Ken raised it over his head and reached for Blue. Blue ducked as Ken swung the net toward him. The net passed harmlessly over his head, but the force of the wind created by the attempt blew the monocle off Blue's eye.

Blue dived over the porch rail, shedding raincoat, hat, and cane in midair. He missed the boat because Billy had it sliding downhill toward the pond, leaving Blue on his own.

Seeing he had missed his chance to net Blue, Ken grabbed a rod fitted with a treble hook and cast it at him, hoping to snag him with the hook.

Rosco saw the weighted hook hit the water, raising a waterspout mere inches behind Blue, where the fish was flopping, wiggling, and squirming in his best getaway gait.

Blue caught the downhill flow of the runoff from the rain and skidded into the pond.

Rosco didn't know what to expect next. But then Ken's shoulders slumped, and he turned back to the house.

Ken picked up his pistol, wiped the water from it, and stepped inside. He motioned for Rosco to follow him in and eased the door closed. He patted Rosco on the head and chuckled.

"Blue didn't exactly look presidential in his retreat, did he? I bet there's a special meeting of the *GWPA* first thing tomorrow morning. But we'll have peace for the rest of the night. Go to sleep, little buddy. And oh, did you notice that I left that floodlight on?" Ken was still laughing when the house lights went out, and Rosco lay down.

Ken was laughing now, but Rosco knew that the master was not in a good mood.  Blue had made a serious error in judgment tonight. The fish thought more of himself than the facts justified.

The battle for Gateway Pond had begun, and Rosco was putting his money on the master.

## The Panther's Challenge

Thursday morning came wet and cold. The rain had stopped, but a heavy mist hung in the air. Rosco was feeling better, but his cough persisted.

Ms. Trudy looked at him and declared that he would stay inside where it was warm and dry. Ken didn't say anything, but Rosco could tell he didn't agree.

After breakfast, Ken pulled on his coat, some heavy boots, and hat and started out the door.

"Where are you going in this weather?" Ms. Trudy asked.

Ken replied, "Wal-Mart. I need a couple of things. Shouldn't be much of a crowd this early in the day. I'll be back soon." He was out the door and gone.

Ms. Trudy had left the laundry room door open. Rosco watched as she sat down in her favorite chair to read and pray. He stood up and trotted over to her.

"Now Rosco, you little rascal, Ken will not like you being in the living room," she said.

Rosco coughed.

Ms. Trudy laughed. "Well, that's right, you are my sick little man. Just lie down here beside the chair while I have my morning quiet time with the Lord."

Rosco lay down at her feet. The house was warm, and the rug was soft under him. He was soon asleep.

A bark awakened Rosco. It was Ginger. She was at the front door, and her bark was one Rosco recognized. It was deep, and it meant danger.

Ms. Trudy knew it, too. She was up and opening the door.

"What is it, girl?" she called to Ginger.

Rosco could see Ginger standing and staring into the woods. The entire posse was there with her.

Ginger looked over her shoulder at Ms. Trudy and wagged her tail, but the hair on her back was still up, and there was a growl in her throat.

A high-pitched shriek answered Ginger's bark. Rosco recognized it as the sound he had heard on that night so long ago when he and his sister had been cast away. It was a big cat. A very big cat.

Ginger and the posse seemed to shrink back. Rosco could tell they feared the cat. He did too. He trotted back to Ms. Trudy's chair and crawled under it.

Ms. Trudy looked at him and then at Ginger. "Stay here, Ginger. Keep the posse on the porch. That was a panther, and I do not want any of you getting hurt."

Ginger and the posse seemed relieved by Ms. Trudy's directions. They gathered together and lay down right in front of the door.

Ms. Trudy closed the door, sat down, and prayed for the safety of Gateway Farm and all the little animals there. She prayed for Ken to come home soon.

Rosco always felt good when he heard Ms. Trudy praying. Her prayers brought peace. But still, he was thankful to be under her chair.

It wasn't long until Rosco heard the sound of Ken's truck. He was so glad the master was home.

Ms. Trudy met Ken at the door and told him about the panther. Rosco saw that the news bothered Ken.

He heard Ken say, "I knew we had a panther close by. I've been seeing his sign. He eats half the kill and covers the rest by pulling leaves over it. Big cats do that so they can return and eat again."

Then Ken said, "I can't let this go any longer. Trying to ignore a problem never works. Roy and I will go looking for him when this weather clears. He will leave this area, or we will have to shoot him. I don't want to, but our animals won't be safe as long as he is this close. Neither will we, for that matter.

In the meantime, let's keep our dogs out of those woods. And it might be best to keep Rosco inside until this is over."

Rosco was thinking, '*No problem here, boss. In fact, how about I stay under this chair?*'

The afternoon passed quietly. Nothing else was heard from the panther, and the tension gradually ebbed away.

Rosco was still under the chair when Ken came in at the end of the day. He listened as Ken called Roy and told him about the panther coming so close to the house earlier that day.

Rosco could hear only Ken's side of the conversation, but he could tell that Roy agreed with Ken. They could not let this go unaddressed. They had to deal with the threat.

Ken ended the call and told Ms. Trudy that Roy would come early the next morning, and the hunt would begin.

Rosco slept under the chair that night. He could smell and hear Ginger and the other dogs as they bedded down on the porch. He could sense their fear as darkness covered the farm.

Rosco woke as the dawn pushed the darkness away. He lay quietly, listening to Ken moving around in his bedroom. He could hear Ginger breathing softly at the front door. All seemed well, and Rosco dozed off again.

Rosco was pulled out of his slumber by the scream of the panther. The malicious disdain of the wild for the domestic filled the room as the big cat hurled his challenge to all takers.

Rosco had jumped, and now he found that he was standing in a puddle of his own making. A whimper escaped as he edged back under the chair. He could hear Ginger and the posse moving around on the porch. He could feel their fear.

Ken walked into the room and opened the front door. He spoke reassuring words to Ginger and then turned to Rosco. "It's all right, boy. He's close, but he won't come out into the open. He knows better. Stay in the house, and you will be safe."

*'You can count on me,'* thought Rosco.

Ken walked back to the bedroom, and when he emerged, he was dressed and carrying a long gun. His face was grim, and Rosco knew the panther's challenge had been accepted. Today the panther would leave and live or fight and die.

Rosco heard a truck and recognized it as Mr. Roy's. He ran to the door as Ken picked up his rifle and stepped out to meet Roy. Rosco saw that Roy had a rifle too.

The two men nodded a greeting to each other, turned away from the house, and walked into the woods. Rosco watched until the deep forest swallowed Ken and Roy.

Ms. Trudy came in, opened the front door, and stepped onto the porch. She lifted her hands to the heavens and prayed, asking the Lord to move the panther on to a place where he could live and hunt without conflict with man and his animals.

She had no more than said her "Amen" when a shot rang out. Then another. The panther's screams bounced off the echo of the shots. Then there was silence.

Rosco had never heard the farm so quiet. It was as if there was no life around them. Not even a whisper from the wind.

Ms. Trudy stood on the porch, and the posse gathered at her feet. Rosco stayed under the chair.

Ginger heard Ken and Roy coming long before they emerged from the woods. She ran to greet them, and the posse followed. Ms. Trudy stepped off the porch. Rosco followed and sat at her feet.

"I heard shots, and then the panthers scream," she said.

"Yes," Ken said. "We saw his tracks almost immediately. He's been sitting there inside the trees, watching the house. I suspect he's intent on taking one of the dogs, probably Rosco. He sees him as prey because he's so little.

"Roy thinks the cat saw us leave the house and was moving enough to stay ahead and out of sight.

We had started down a steep creek bank when the leaves rustled. We looked up, and there he stood above us on the opposite bank.

Then Roy raised his rifle and fired a round into the air. We only wanted to warn him and scare him into leaving the area so we wouldn't have to kill him.

But he just stood there without flinching. He raised his head and let out a scream. Clearly, he had laid claim not only to the forest but also to the farm itself. He intended to rule by the force of intimidation. There would be no compromise.

I took a shot at him. As I fired, he jumped sideways. I thought I hit him and was waiting for him to fall, but he stared at me with those green eyes full of hate, turned, and bounded into the brush and was gone."

"Do you think he'll be back?" Ms. Trudy asked.

"We just don't know." "Time will tell, but based on his actions, he has no fear of guns and no respect for mankind. I'd say he has staked out these woods as his domain and intends to stay."

## The Battle For Gateway Pond

The rain moved out, and as the sky cleared, an Indian summer settled over Gateway Farm. Rosco moved from under Ms. Trudy's chair to the front porch, where he lay in the warming sun, and gradually the cough left his body. It was on the porch where Ken found Rosco late one December afternoon.

"I am going down to the dock to deal with that pesky blue catfish. Want to go and watch me catch him?" Ken asked.

Rosco was up in a flash. He could see that Ken had his fishing rod in one hand and the other held a bag of something that smelled like fish but different. He sniffed it.

"That's shrimp. I bought it the other day when I went to Wal-Mart. I had to keep it in the freezer while we dealt with the panther and waited for the weather to clear. I don't like to use frozen shrimp, but I'm so ready to get that troublemaking blue catfish out of the pond that I'm going to make an exception. Let's go get it done, boy," Ken said as he turned to walk toward the pond.

Rosco ran along beside him. *Man, oh, man! This was going to be something to see.*

He watched as Ken baited his hook with a large piece of frozen shrimp and cast it far out into the middle of the pond. Ken nodded his satisfaction with the results of the cast and sat down in a folding chair he had brought along.

"Perfect," Ken said. "I won't be long, and every fish in the pond will be smelling that shrimp. Blue too.

Being the bully that he is, he will run all the others away and claim it as his. Hope he swallows it whole, hook and all."

Ken had no more spoken than the bobber went under, the line became taut, and the reel began to sing as the shrimp was carried to the bottom of the pond.

"It's Blue!" Ken shouted as he jumped out of his chair and grabbed the rod. "He's got the shrimp and is diving for the deep. Next, he will roll and try to wrap the line around a stump or something to break it. But I got him on a twenty-five-pound test line, and he's mine for sure."

Just as suddenly as it began, it was over. Blue arched up and out of the water, turned to face the dock, and spit the shrimp, hook and all, at Ken. It hit the dock, bounced once, and landed in front of Ken's right boot.

Blue hit the water in his patented cannonball dive, sending a wall of smelly pond water up in a wave that descended where Ken was standing. It flooded over him from head to foot.

Ken dropped his pole and gasped at the shock of the cold December shower, sucking in the nasty pond water. The taste gagged him, and he bent over, retching and stumbling forward. As he did, he stepped on the shrimp sending the hook through the sole of his boot and into his big toe.

Ken screamed in pain and lurched sideways, lifting his foot to take the pressure off the toe. Ken was hooked.

Rosco feared Ken was about to fall off the dock and into the pond. Blue thought so, too, and was eagerly awaiting the opportunity to get Ken into his realm.

At the last moment, Ken grabbed the rail on the dock and pulled himself back and onto solid footing.

Rosco could see the pain on Ken's face. He sat down and considered how to get the boot off, so he could get the hook out of his big toe. Ken opened the tackle box, removed a pair of wire nippers, and cut the line from the hook.

He retrieved his pocketknife from his jeans, opened it, and cut the boot down the side from the top all the way to the heel. Then, he cut it along the side nearly to where the hook entered the sole of the boot. He sawed down and through the sole, opening the boot to expose the hook.

Ken slipped the boot off, wincing and crying in pain as the boot scraped against the shank of the hook still embedded in his big toe.

Ken's face glistened with sweat. Blood had soaked through his sock. Ken gingerly used the nippers to cut the sock away from the hook and off his foot.

Rosco watched as Ken took a deep breath and lightly grasped the exposed shank of the hook with the nippers. He heard Ken gasp and watched as he bent over, rocking back and forth. Rosco knew he was hurting.

"I can't stand the pain," Ken said. "That barb is set deeply in my toe. A doctor will have to cut this hook out.

I have to get to the house, Rosco; but I'm not sure I can make it. Suppose you run up there and bark. See if you can get Ms. Trudy's attention. Run back this way barking, and she will know something is wrong. Can you do that, boy?"

Rosco was gone in a flash. He was barking as he hit the porch. He ran to the door, barking and scratching on it.

Ms. Trudy opened it and said, "Oh my goodness, Rosco. What's wrong, boy?"

Rosco jumped from the porch and ran toward the dock barking and looking back at Ms. Trudy. She stepped from the porch and looked toward the pond. Ken saw her and waved for her to come to him.

"Something's wrong with my Ken," Rosco heard her say.

Ms. Trudy ran back into the house and emerged with the keys to the golf cart. Rosco jumped onto the seat beside her as she drove to the dock.

Ms. Trudy took one look at Ken's foot and said, "Oh, my. We must get you to the doctor!"

Rosco watched helplessly as Ms. Trudy struggled to get Ken into the cart. Ken cried out with each step, but finally, he was in the cart. Rosco jumped in beside him and licked his hand.

When they got to the house, Ms. Trudy told Ken to wait as she got her car keys and purse. She ran into the house and came back outside as Roy drove up.

Roy took it all in quickly. He and Ms. Trudy helped Ken out of the cart and into her car. Rosco jumped in, too.

Rosco waited in the car at the doctor's office while Ms. Trudy took Ken inside.

The door barely closed behind them before Rosco realized he needed to pee. Oh no, he thought. Not in the car. Ms. Trudy will be so upset with me.

He jumped from the seat to the floorboard and settled down to wait, being as still as he could, hoping he could hold his water. After what seemed an eternity, the car door opened, and there was Ms. Trudy with Ken in a chair that had wheels on it.

Rosco jumped out of the car and ran to the front tire. He lifted his leg and watched over his shoulder as Ms. Trudy and a nurse helped Ken into the vehicle.

"Rosco! That's so rude," Ms. Trudy scolded. "I'm so disappointed in you, doing that right here in the doctor's parking lot and on the tire of my car."

*'Well, you'd be a lot more disappointed if I had wet your seats,'* thought Rosco.

At home, Roy helped Ms. Trudy get Ken into the house. They helped him sit down and put his foot on the coffee table. He didn't notice that Rosco had followed along and was now sitting beside his chair.

"I know it hurts," Roy said. "How in the world did you get a hook in your toe? Didn't you have boots on?"

"Long story, better suited for another day," Ken replied.

"Right," Roy said. "Bet Blue had something to do with this, and can't wait to hear all about it."

Ken stayed in the house for most of the next week with his foot on Ms. Trudy's table. Rosco noticed that Ms. Trudy didn't seem to mind Ken having his foot on the table the first few days.

As time passed and he got better, she started to fuss at him about taking his foot off her coffee table, saying it would be best for him to put his foot down and let the blood flow return to that toe.

After one such criticism, Ken looked at Rosco and said, "Rosco, it looks like we've ridden this horse about as far as it will take us. I guess it's time to get up and get out."

Rosco watched as Ken limped down the hall toward his bedroom. When he came back, Rosco could not believe his eyes. Ken had his boots on. He was wearing his fishing glasses, and his hat was in his hand. This meant one thing and one thing only. Ken was going back for Blue.

"Now, Ken," Ms. Trudy said. "You are not going down to that dock. Take those glasses off and sit on the porch for a while. That fish is not worth all this fuss."

Ken said nothing. Not one thing. He limped through the house and onto the porch and picked up his fishing pole. Rosco watched Ken open his tackle box and place a pack of stink bait inside.

"Want to see the show, boy?" Ken said to Rosco.

*'Yep, for sure. Here we go again,'* Rosco thought.

Ken drove the golf cart to the barn, dismounted, and walked to the tack room. Rosco watched as Ken removed his biggest rope and fastened it to the cable-loaded winch mounted to the front of the big Ford tractor.

Ken picked up his fishing gear and tied it to the back of the tractor's seat. Then he picked Rosco up and climbed onto the tractor. He settled Rosco in his lap and drove the tractor to the pond.

Rosco knew Ken didn't like to drive the tractor to the pond when he was going to fish because he said the fish could hear and feel the vehicle coming. Ken said the sound and vibration put them on their guard, and getting them to take the bait was harder.

Something was up, and Rosco was betting it had to do with Blue's stump.

At the dock, Ken stepped from the tractor and walked onto the dock with the rope in his hand. He coiled the rope and laid it on the dock beside his chair. Ken baited a hook, and this time, he cast it to sink beside Blue's stump.

"That'll bring the rascal," Ken said.

Sure enough, not much time passed before there was a ripple in the water, and Blue jumped out of the water and onto his stump. He wiggled and flopped around until he was able to stand up on his tail fin.

Rosco saw he was leaning on a dry reed, using it as a cane, like he had that night up at the house. Ken had seen him too, but he sat quietly in his folding chair.

Blue just wallowed around on the stump staring at Ken across the pond.

Rosco could hear that teapot sound escaping from between Ken's clenched teeth. He knew this was going to go bad quickly. He backed up a couple of steps and sat down. Blue was pushing it.

By now, heads had popped up all around the stump as the pond residents gathered to watch this exchange between Blue and Ken. *'They might be a tad too close to Blue and that stump,'* Rosco thought, but he held his peace and watched.

Blue was playing to the crowd.

There was splashing in the shallows under the big pecan tree, and Rosco turned to look that way. Four of the biggest turtles Rosco had ever seen crawled halfway up the bank to rest at an angle to the dock where Ken sat.

Each one had mud smeared on their shells. Rosco leaned forward and focused. Then he realized what he was seeing. The mud formed letters. There was one on each turtle's back. Put together; they formed *GPCA*. Rosco heard Ken gasp as he deciphered the acronym. Gateway Pond Citizens' Association.

Blue turned and bowed to his fans, who had broken into a celebration. They were all splashing and exchanging high fins.

Rosco saw Ken's face flush, with red spots creeping up his throat all the way to his forehead. Rosco knew Blue had pushed Ken over the edge.

But Blue was so busy bowing and egging on the crowd that he never saw Ken come out of the chair, rope in hand.

But Blue heard him as Ken bellowed, "Why you bubble-headed, bug-eyed, big-mouthed, bewhiskered blue devil."

Rosco watched as Ken twirled the rope over his head and cast it for the stump where Blue was standing.

The rest of what Ken had to say was lost to Rosco as he turned to watch the rope settle neatly over the stump.

Blue seemed frozen by the suddenness of Ken's actions. Rosco watched as the fish stood there, mouth open, as the rope sailed up and over. This seemed to jar him into the realization that he was in the direct path of the rope and his best interest was not served by remaining on his stump.

Blue arched up and off the stump in a blur, diving for Davey Jones's locker. Blue was beneath the waves, but Ken had his stump roped.

Rosco watched as Ken walked to the tractor and activated the winch. The rope drew tight and hesitated as the stump resisted its pull. But then, the irresistible force overcame the immovable object. The stump had sat in the water for twenty years or more and was weakened by rot.

First came a great sigh as its roots gave way, and it was pulled from the muddy moorings of its youth. Then up and out, it came, leaving nothing but a few muddy bubbles. The remains of a once-proud tree were no more.

The stump would never lure another squirrel nor serve again as the stage for Blue's political rabblerousing.

'*What now?*' Rosco wondered.

Ken looked at Rosco and said, "No more stage for Blue, Rosco. Blue thought I was trying to rope him. Not so.

I planned to catch Blue and move him out of this big pond into the little one, where he would not be able to cause so much trouble, then to come back and pull his stump. But when he climbed onto that stump and started playing to the crowd, I decided it was time to stop the show and destroy his stage. As it worked out, this was the better way to do it."

Ken went on, "The stump was too far from the bank to reach with a sledgehammer, and it was too low in the water to me to boat out and use a chainsaw on it. It has been in the water for twenty years or better, and while it still supported Blue, I knew it was rotted enough that it would quickly give way to the pull of the winch.

Just before I threw the rope, I realized that Blue was going to jump from the stump, but I never planned on him diving into the water in the exact spot where I cast the stink bait. But he did, and you know what I think happened, Rosco? I believe Blue left that stump in such a hurry that he forgot the hook was in the water on that side. I bet you a steak dinner that he landed on the hook and is now caught, sure as Jake.

Look here. See how tight this line is? Something is caught on it, and I'm saying it's Blue."

Rosco looked as Ken picked up the pole and started to reel in the line. *Yep, something was hooked. Rosco was hoping it wasn't Blue because as much as he disliked the loudmouth, he wanted Ken to be wrong so he'd have to feed Rosco that steak dinner.* He licked his lips as he thought about the bone.

"Well, look at what we have here. It's Big Blue all tangled up and with my hook firmly planted in his tail fin. How does it feel, Mr. President?" Ken laughed.

Rosco watched as Ken hoisted Blue out of the water and onto the dock. He could see that Ken was right. In his haste to escape the mayhem of his own creation, Blue had dived onto the hook where it hung suspended in the water. The razor-sharp point had pierced his tail.

Rosco could imagine Blue's frantic efforts to shake the hook, rolling and spinning as catfish do. But this time, it hadn't worked. The barb at the end of the hook had him snared. The more he rolled, the more entangled he became in Ken's twenty-five-pound line. His panic resulted in this, and he was now laying on the dock helplessly hooked and gasping for breath.

Ken sat in his chair and looked at Blue. "You know, Blue, by the right of victory, I should fry you up and serve you at the next social. But I have never intended you harm. So, I will tell you what I'm going to do.

First, I'm going to put you in this wire basket and drop you over the side so you can catch your breath. Then I'm going to bring you up and make you an offer that I don't think you will refuse."

Rosco watched as Ken dropped Blue down into the pond. Blue stopped struggling as the water covered his gills and the life-giving breath returned. After a few minutes, Ken lifted him up and sat him down on the dock.

"Better, Blue? OK, here's my offer, and you get only one chance to respond. As I said before, I bear no malice nor want any harm to come to you. But I cannot allow this rabblerousing to continue. So, I propose to move you from the big pond to the little pond, where you will have less opportunity to rally support and raise a rebellion against the natural order of things.

And just in case you don't know, the natural order of things that I refer to holds that mankind is superior and appointed to rule over the birds of the air, the fish of the waters, and the animals of the land. In the beginning, it was given to us to subdue and have dominion. It is ours to guide, to guard, and to govern. I intend to be obedient to that commission," Ken paused and looked at Blue.

"Now, that does not mean that I should subject you to mistreatment or deny you the right to life, liberty, and the pursuit of happiness. And I will not.

I will be fair. I will meet my obligations as the steward of Gateway Farm and all of the inhabitants thereof. As far as possible, I will remain at peace with all I come into contact with. That includes you, Blue," Ken paused again, dropped Blue back into the pond for a few minutes, and brought him back up and onto the dock.

"There it is, Blue. If I have your word that you will stop the rabblerousing and live in peace with your fellow creatures and with me, then you will go to the small pond today. If not, you will go into the frying pan tomorrow. What do you say?" Ken said and sat, waiting for Blue to respond.

Blue coughed and rolled his eyes up to stare at Ken. There was malice in those eyes.

Ken took a deep breath and said, "Somehow, some way, you have missed the point here. This is not an opportunity to escape the pan and live to fight another day. This war is over. And while I'm at it, let me correct one other misconception you seem to hold. You have no public. Understand? You are a blue catfish, period.

I am not sure you get it, but I will give you the benefit of the doubt and release you into the little pond. But Blue, you mark my words. There will be a much different ending if I have to come after you again."

Blue squirmed violently, trying to escape back into the safety of the pond's deep water.

Ken held him tight and laughed, "No, sir. The talking is over, and the battle for Gateway Pond is finished. I won; you lost."

Rosco followed as Ken walked across the pasture and gently released Blue into the small pond. Blue swam out a few feet and turned to gaze at Ken.

He whipped around and flipped his tail, sending a spray of water out and over Ken. And then he disappeared into the deep water.

Rosco was amazed by Blue's action, but he was more amazed when Ken, dripping wet, laughed and turned away.

"Come on, Rosco Jack. That ends the battle for Gateway Pond. Now, if that panther does not return, we should have peace on the farm." Ken bent over and pulled on Rosco's ears.

Rosco wanted to share Ken's joy, but the question of the panther's return remained.

## Out of the House

December passed, and January came. The snow returned with the New Year and the coldest weather Rosco had yet to experience.

Ms. Trudy kept him in the house day and night, letting him out to take care of his business. Those were quick trips, indeed. Rosco hated wading through the snow.

The cold penetrated his bones, and he found himself wet and shaking from each trip outside. The only thing good about these forays was that Ms. Trudy always greeted him with a soft, fluffy towel, warm from the dryer. She would rub and dry his fur while talking sweetly to him. Rosco knew she loved him, and he adored her.

Day after dreary day was followed by night after a long, cold night. Rosco would lie on his blankets in the laundry room and listen to the wind driving the sleet and rain against the door. Often the door would be sealed with a gasket of ice when Ken opened it for the morning feeding.

Rosco would stand out of sight, but he knew the posse could smell him, and he knew they resented his being in the warm, dry house while they had to sleep in the barn.

Ken often suggested to Ms. Trudy that Rosco needed to be in the barn with the rest of the dogs, but she always put a quick end to those conversations.

"Not on your life, Ken Bangs," Ms. Trudy would say. "Those are big dogs, full-grown with thick coats of fur. Rosco weighs six pounds. He's still a puppy and is a shorthaired Jack Russell.

He would freeze out there if one of the coyotes didn't eat him first. No sir. Rosco stays inside through the winter, and that's all we need to say on this subject."

Rosco could see that Ken disagreed, but he could also see the matter was settled. Rosco Jack heaved a deep sigh, turned in a tight circle, and lay down on his soft, warm blankets.

Ken closed the door and trooped off to the barn to be sure the posse had clean straw to sleep on, fresh water to drink, and plenty of food to eat. Ken liked to say the winter winds swept through the barn's open aisle *"like Grant through Georgia."*

He would pull bales of hay out of the loft and stack them, two high, in a horseshoe design around the posse's sleeping area. The barn kept the dogs dry, and the hay blocked the wind. The dogs huddled together, sharing each other's body heat. That and their thick coats of fur kept them warm.

Ken thought Rosco would benefit from learning how to survive in nature. He knew the lessons of life for a dog were best learned from other dogs. But Ms. Trudy had adopted Rosco as her *"little man,"* and Ken would have to wait until spring. Then, he would take Rosco from the house and release him into Ginger's care. She would turn him into what he was meant to be, a farm dog and a full member of the Gateway Posse.

Spring came and with it the warming south winds to melt the snow and dry the wet grounds. Rosco would scratch at the door until Ms. Trudy let him out, firmly stating, "Don't you get off the porch, Rosco. You are so little I'm afraid something will eat you. I could not stand it if anything happened to my little man."

She would stand and watch until Rosco trotted over to his favorite patch of sunbeams and lay down. Then she would go back inside and close the door.

Rosco loved lying stretched out in the sun, feeling it loosen his muscles and warm his bones to the very marrow. He loved the sights and smells of spring, and he loved to watch the posse romping and playing on the farm. He wanted to join them, but Ms. Trudy had said something about him being eaten. That and the sight of the big hawks sweeping low across the pastures was enough to keep him on the porch.

And that's the way the days passed through March and April. The April rains ended, the earth was alive with brilliantly colored flowers, and May brought a stirring in Rosco that he could no longer deny.

There was a strong desire to run with the posse, a compulsion that eventually overcame his fear of being eaten. Then, one morning it drove him off of the porch and sent him running to join the posse as they headed to the forest.

Ginger heard his bark and turned to wait for him. The posse waited with her.

Rosco saw the new dog that had come to the farm during the winter. He was as tall as Ginger, muscular, and thick through the chest. He had a broad face and intelligent eyes and stood with quiet yet regal confidence. Rosco had heard Ken say he was a pit bull and looked like an excellent addition to the posse.

He had come to the farm after his family had moved away and left him tied to the porch of their abandoned house. By the time he'd chewed through the rope, he was half-starved and desperate for water.

Ken had seen him standing beside the road, drinking muddy water from the ditch. He still had the rope around his neck.

Stopping his truck, Ken approached him with a soft voice, loving words, and gentle hands. The dog sensed the man was safe and stood still.

Slowly removing the rope, Ken saw open wounds where the dog had tried to escape the choking restraint. He coaxed the dog into his truck and drove with him to the farm.

Ken opened the truck's door and, gathering the weak dog in his arms; carried him into the barn. There he had cleaned the wounds around the dog's neck with a gentle disinfectant and then coated them with an antibiotic salve. He fed and watered the dog and left him to get acquainted with the posse.

The next day, Ken returned to the barn and brushed the snarls and burs out of the big dog's coat. The posse had accepted him, and Ken could tell the dog felt safe.

Ken named him Rusty because of his red coat. Rosco liked Rusty immediately.

Ginger sniffed Rosco and stepped back. She watched as each dog sniffed his or her acceptance of Rosco. But Ginger was their leader, and it was her decision to make.

Rosco stood still and quiet with his head held high. Would she allow him to join them, or was he still too little?

Ginger turned and led the way into the forest. Rosco strode alongside Rusty. Rosco was out of the house, off the porch, and with the posse. Now his training would begin.

Ginger led the posse up hills, down gullies, across creeks, and through briar patches. They examined every foot of their domain, marking their territory by leaving notice of their presence along the way.

Rosco saw wild hogs using their snouts to push up and consume tender roots, snakes sunning on exposed rocks, deer grazing on the tender new growth along the creeks, rabbits scurrying away at their approach and hawks floating on the wind and then darting down to swoop up a careless mouse. He saw squirrels, too.

Each squirrel seemed to know of his humiliation last fall and shared it across the forest in an incessant chattering from the treetops. Painful as it was, Rosco knew he had no one to blame but himself.

For a while, he had blamed Collins. But gradually, he had come to accept that he and he alone was responsible for his actions.

He had heard Ken tell one of the young men who lived at Gateway that being a male was a matter of birth, but being a man was a matter of choice. Males become men when they choose to accept and deal with the consequences of their actions.

That resonated with Rosco. He remembered what Ken had said to Blue about mankind being chosen to exercise dominion over the earth, and he knew that he was a dog, not a man.

Still, he had determined that having been born a male, and a small one at that, he would live his life as near as possible to the principles of manhood.

He would exercise care in selecting his friends, knowing that he would be influenced by and marked as one of those with whom he associated. He knew that his decision to remain on the farm rather than leave with Collins had been right. He was glad to be running with the posse.

The posse ran easily for hours. Then, Rosco felt a change. The posse had tensed up, slowing their pace and testing the air with their keen sense of smell. He lifted his nose and sniffed. There it was, the smell of the big cat. It was as strong as it had been on that first night.

Ginger dropped to the ground. The posse followed suit. Rosco watched as Ginger looked back, communicating with the posse to wait while she scouted this out.

She crawled forward on her belly. Her ears were straight up, and Rosco could see that she was monitoring sound by the way she was moving them, using them as if they were directional finders. Then she stopped.

Ginger looked back, and the pack moved forward. There, just across a small creek, was a shallow cave. Rosco could tell that the floods that came each spring had hollowed it out.

Staring at him from the darkness of the cave were those green eyes that haunted his dreams. Rosco drew back. The rest of the posse lay still, awaiting Ginger's move. The panther growled softly but waited also.

Rosco could see that the big cat was hurt. Ken had not missed his shot so long ago. The bullet had hit him behind his left shoulder and had turned down, bouncing off a rib and exiting in front of his left hip. A ragged furrow marked the bullet's path.

He had lost a lot of weight, and the long, cold winter had taken its toll on his strength. The brilliant green eyes were now dulled, and he panted heavily, even as he lay flat on the ground.

Ginger stood slowly. The panther's eyes never left her as she moved up and down along the bank. She found what she was looking for, tracks from another big cat, this one a female.

Ginger had suspected as much. The male could not have survived the winter alone with that wound. The female had killed and brought food to the male as evidenced by the bones strewn around the cave. Her body warmth had kept him from freezing. He was going to survive, but he was still too weak to hunt.

Ginger knew the female would not venture far from the wounded male, and her return was sure. Ginger sniffed the panther's tracks and knew that the female had not been gone long. She was staying close and would be back soon.

It was time to leave. Ginger looked the panther over again, then turned and led the posse away at a fast pace. She maintained the pace until she was sure they had traveled far enough to be safe. The female would not follow them far.

Rosco found it easy to keep up with the posse, and he took comfort in the fact that Rusty seemed to have adopted him as a little brother. He knew Rusty would defend him, and that gave him comfort.

Ginger stopped as they came to a broad, quickly flowing stream. Given the swift current, she looked around at Rosco as she considered whether he could make it across.

She turned and moved beside the stream until it curved back to the north. There she found the stream bridged by a fallen tree, a victim of the winter storms. It was wide and provided solid footing as she led her posse across, then turned to drink deeply of the cold, fresh water.

She lingered a moment, letting each dog drink their fill. Then, lifting her nose, she sniffed the air, checking for danger. Finding none but still wary of the two big cats in her woods, she turned toward home. Dusk found them exiting the forest and heading to the barn.

Ginger looked back to see if Rosco would turn toward the house or stay with the posse. There he was, trotting along beside Rusty. His little tongue was hanging out of his mouth, and his gait had slowed, but he stayed with them right to the barn.

Ginger checked each of her charges, sniffing and licking to be sure each was okay. When she came to Rosco, she found him asleep; he had fallen where he'd stopped. Ginger stood looking at him. He was with them now. Rosco was out of the house.

## The Overflow

Deep in the night, a cold rain began to fall. Rosco woke as the heavy drops penetrated his thin fur bringing a chill that caused tremors to shake him.

Struggling against the protest of stiff muscles, he limped inside the barn on feet sore from the previous day's hours of running with the posse. Stepping over to Gracie and Mercie, he settled down next to Rusty and was instantly asleep again.

The rainfall continued throughout the night, and by morning it was pounding down, tattooing its rhythm on the barn's tin roof. The posse woke to the sound of men's voices.

"How much rain have we had?" Pete asked Larry.

"I am not sure, but it has been raining hard since midnight," Larry replied.

"We better check the earthen dam on the far end of the big pond. The ground was already saturated. Now we've had all this runoff into a pond that was full to start with," Pete said.

"You worried that the dam might not hold, Pete?"

"I looked at it before I went in last night. The water was a couple of feet from the top. There is not much doubt that all this rain will send it over the top, and the added pressure could well break the dam," Pete replied.

"Did you look at the little pond?" Larry asked.

"Yep. It was already out of the banks last night. It's probably running into the big pond this morning. That will add to the problem," Pete said.

Rosco listened to the men talk. His mind was already at work figuring out what all this meant. For starters, if the little pond was now overflowing into the big pond, could Blue escape his exile and return to his public? And what about the Panthers?

Rosco's mind brought up the image of the cave the cats had adapted into a den. It sat a few feet above the surface of the stream. By now, the overflowing stream would have turned into a raging torrent.

Rosco knew cats hated to be wet. Reason dictated they had been flushed out. They would be searching for a dry place to wait out the storm. But where? Two thousand acres of forest surrounded Gateway Farm, and every foot of it was awash in the flood that continued even now.

Rosco knew the answer. The only place the Panthers could escape the rain was the farm. They would be seeking shelter in one of the outbuildings. Rosco was sure of that.

Trouble was riding in on the waves of this storm. Gateway Farm would be fortunate if all that came was the rain's overflow.

The rain slowed around noon. By this time, hunger had overcome the desire to stay dry, and the posse was restless. They were milling around the front of the barn when Ken's voice rang out, calling them to the house to eat.

They surged from the barn, through the light rain, and onto the porch, where Ken had set out bowls full of food covered in warm milk. Tails wagged as the bowls were emptied and licked clean.

Ken laughed and said, "Well, thanks, boys and girls, for doing the dishes for me. The rain has picked up again, so why don't you all stay here on the porch rather than getting soaked going back to the barn? The weather forecast says it should stop raining in a couple of hours. Then we will check the ponds and the cattle in the lower pasture. They are probably all huddled up in their shelters. I sure hope the water has not gotten into the shelters."

The posse lay down. Their full bellies and the sound of the rain on the roof soon had them all sleeping.

Hours passed, and the rain continued to fall. Ken came out and looked at the sky and then at the water flooding the farm. Rosco could see that he was worried.

Rosco noticed that Ken had his rain suit and high-topped boots on. He also had one of the walkie-talkies that he used to talk with the men who helped him work the farm.

Ken lifted the radio and spoke into it. "Pete, Larry, do you copy me?"

"Go ahead, Ken, we're both here at the shop," came Larry's reply.

"It doesn't look like this rain is going to stop anytime soon. I'm worried about the dam and the cows in the lower pasture. Bring that big-wheeled Gator and some shovels and meet me on the far end of the dam. I want to be sure those overflow pipes are open so we can let as much water as possible flow downstream."

"Roger, that. We're on our way," Larry responded.

"Better slip your radios in a plastic bag, or this rain will ruin them," Ken said.

"Got it," Larry answered.

Rosco watched Ken put his radio into a plastic bag, as he had suggested to Larry and Pete. He then stepped off the porch and onto a Big Bear four-wheeler. He turned it towards the pond, and the posse followed.

The rain had pushed the pond beyond the banks, and it was flowing over the dam. Ken had to leave the four-wheeler and walk.

The water got deeper as they got closer to the dam. They could hear the roar of the water rushing out of the pond through the overflow pipes on the far end of the barrier.

Pete and Larry arrived in the Gator, and Rosco saw they had taken time to tie the rowboat onto the Gator. They now set it off, got into the boat, and paddled to Ken.

"That is a great idea," Ken said.

"I don't think it's safe for the three of us to be on foot in this moving water. Pete and I will paddle over to the pipes and be sure they're open and free running," Larry said.

Ken nodded and said, "I'll check the cows while you do that. Take care not to get caught in that current, or it'll wash you downstream all the way to Lake Wright Patman."

"I know, that's right," laughed Larry.

Rosco and the posse sat still as Ken turned to wade towards the lower pasture. A flash in the water caught their attention.

"What was that?" Ken asked.

"It was Blue," Pete said.

"Did you see him?" Ken asked.

"Yes. I can still see him. He is hanging at the edge of the current, about three feet to the right of the intake on the overflow pipe," Pete was pointing to Blue.

Ken stood looking at Blue. Apparently, he had washed out of the little pond, and the overflow had carried him across the pasture and into the big pond. He was floating there, holding steady against the current. It was as though he wanted to be seen.

He leaped from the water and landed in front of the drain in a perfect dive, not two feet from where they were standing. He paused a minute, flipped his tail, sending a spray over them, and disappeared under the rushing water.

"What do you make of that?" Ken asked.

Larry stood thinking, and Pete said, "I will tell you what I think. Blue just sent a message. He was saying these ponds couldn't hold him. The overflow gave him a way out, and he's going to ride it to the big water at Lake Wright Patman.

I will bet you a dollar to a donut that we can boat up after this flood subsides and find him there, where this stream enters the lake. I will bet you again that he'll be waiting there with a whole new following, ready and eager to wage war, man against fish.

He thinks he can beat you, Boss, and he wants to do so in front of a much larger crowd than he can gather here in the ponds. That's what I think, but the question is, what do you think?"

"What are you going to do?" Larry asked.

"About what?" Ken asked.

"About that obnoxious catfish," Pete said.

"Oh, he's right. The war is not over, because he does not want it to be over. We will meet again one day, and when we do, I'll have fried catfish for dinner that night. But right now, I need to check on those cows," Ken said.

Ken climbed through the fence and walked down the slope into the lower pasture. As he walked around the first stand of trees, he could see the water was deep enough to cover the lower half of his boots, and it was flowing fast.

Ken stood still, considering the scene for a minute.

He decided he could make it across and over the next little rise, where he would be able to look directly into the shelter and see the cows.

He waded through the rushing water to the higher ground. He looked into the lower pasture and was surprised to see all the cows standing belly-deep in the stream's rushing water.

*"Why are they not in the shelter? It will provide them relief from this pounding rain,"* Ken wondered.

He worked his way around behind them and started herding them toward the shelter. But they shied away and turned back. Ken called for Ginger and the posse to help.

Ginger led the way, and the posse circled the cows to move them toward the shelter. As they drew close, the cows broke away again, running from the shelter.

At that instant, Rosco knew. The Panthers were there. His hair stood up on his neck, and he began to growl.

"What is it, boy?" Ken asked. His answer was the panther's roar.

Ken turned to look at the shelter. He was too close to the shelter and would never be able to outrun the Panthers. He knew that he was in mortal danger.

Ken always carried a pistol when he left the house. Today, he had the Browning nine-millimeter that he had carried as a police officer. He named her *Lady Justice.*

He had *Lady Justice* loaded with super velocity hollow points.

These rounds were designed for self-defense and would stop most threats on the farm, but he doubted they would protect him against an animal the size of a Panther.

But the pistol was all he had. If he had to shoot the Panthers, his shots would have to be perfectly placed.

Ken removed the pistol from under his rain suit and faced the shelter. There was water, not much but some, in the bottom of the shelter. Ken lifted his eyes to look into the loft. He saw both of the Panthers. They were watching him intently and were poised, ready to jump.

The cats had climbed into the hayloft to escape the water covering the floor of the shelter. The male stood as he detected Ken's smell. He recognized that smell as coming from the man who had shot him.

Hatred filled the big cat. He was not fully healed, but it was time to settle the score.

Bunching himself, the panther launched out from the loft and toward Ken. Ken had anticipated the move.

He lifted *Lady Justice* and put two quick rounds in the cat's head. They struck the cat hard, and he fell at Ken's feet.

The cat's lips curled back in a snarl as hatred for the man washed away the pain. Ken read on his face that he was coming again. Not waiting, Ken put two more rounds between the cat's hate-filled eyes. The cat died there in the overflow that had driven him from the forest into man's domain.

Ken stood over the body, thinking what a waste it was. This was the price of the pride that had led this magnificent animal, against all reason, into harm's way. This was the result of the hatred that had filled his heart.

Ken turned back to the loft. The female stood watching Ken. She was twitching her tail. Ken could read her mind. She had chosen flight over fight. '*Good decision. Get gone, girl,*' he thought.

The next instant, she was in the air. Unlike the male, she was neither wounded nor weak. She was in the prime of her life. She stretched her body flat and flew like a tawny lance directly over Ken's head.

He turned to watch her smooth flight and saw her gather herself so she would land on her feet. As soon as she touched down, she was running flat out.

And there was Rosco, directly in front of her. Ken could see his face and guessed what was about to happen.

Rosco was focused on the big cat in front of him. This was one of those who had denied his sister the right to life. The cat was the embodiment of the fear that had tormented him in dreams of that night so long ago. It was time to face the fear and to remove her as a threat to others, once and for all.

The posse was on the cat's heels, and their baying told her that even the slightest pause to deal with this pesky runt in front of her would mean severe injury or possibly death. Her best hope was to try and escape.

Ken watched. He knew a fight was coming. He knew it would go badly for his dogs.

He lifted the pistol but then let it drop. He could not risk a shot because the posse was so close behind her, and Rosco was in the line of fire. He could do nothing but watch. The scene seemed to unfold in slow motion, but it happened in a flash.

The panther bounded up, intending to jump over Rosco and escape down the draw and into the forest. But the saturated ground gave way, and she slipped, falling onto her side.

Rosco hit her full in the face. She screamed as he sunk his needle-sharp teeth deep into her right eye, rupturing it and blinding her in that eye.

A shake of her head sent him splashing across the pasture, but the delay he had caused in her flight allowed the posse to catch up.

They were on her in a fury. She matched them tooth and nail.

Rusty surged in from her blindside and locked onto her throat. He ripped down and out. Blood spewed from the wound as she turned on him and broke his neck with one powerful swipe of her right paw.

Ginger sprang forward, locking onto the back of her neck. The cat roared in pain, but she could not reach nor dislodge Ginger despite her best efforts. Ginger knew this and held on, increasing the pressure with each opportunity.

Her desperate efforts to dislodge Ginger allowed the remaining dogs to get into the fight.

Gracie ran straight in and ripped the cat's left front shoulder, slashing deep and retreating in time to avoid a crushing sweep of the mighty right paw.

Mercie dodged back to the right, taking advantage of the cat's blind spot, and went for her throat. She locked onto the wound Rusty had opened.

Like Rusty, she too slashed down and ripped out, turning the wound into a gaping hole. This time the blood was thick and deep red. It issued forth in spurts.

Mercie had opened the jugular. It was a mortal wound, and the cat knew it. But death had not claimed her yet.

In a burst of fury, she whirled and took the back of Mercie's neck in her mouth. With a violent twist, she snapped the neck and flung Mercie's body aside.

Bo lunged in, hitting her shoulder high and knocking her off her feet and onto her back. He rode her as she rolled over, slashing at her with his teeth.

The big cat reached up with her hind legs from flat on her back. Ken saw the razor-sharp claws being extended and could do nothing as she raked them down Bo's exposed underside. She opened him from chest to belly, and he bled out, falling dead at the panther's feet.

The force of Bo's collision had dislodged and stunned Ginger. The dying panther had one strike left. Slapping with her left paw, she opened a six-inch gash in Ginger's hip. She snarled once more and died with her claws still embedded in Ginger's flesh.

Ken stood looking at the scene. His heart was broken. Bo, Rusty, and Mercie lay dead. Ginger was severely wounded. Only Rosco and Gracie were unscathed.

A high price had been paid. But the farm and its' occupants were now free of the danger, the encroachment of those who refused to live in peace with their fellow creatures. The posse had defended their home and family.

Ken heard Ginger whimper and turned to see Rosco and Gracie standing over her, licking her wound. Ken walked over and patted both dogs. He removed the panther's claws from Ginger's hip. He picked Ginger up and carried her out of the lower pasture and toward the pond.

Larry and Pete had heard the battle and were running toward him. They took Ginger from him, carried her to the Gator and drove her to the barn.

Ken laid Ginger on a pallet of clean straw and examined her wound. It was deep and long but clean, and the cat had not cut any muscle or blood vessels.

He cleaned it with hydrogen peroxide then applied an antibiotic salve. A visit to the vet for a once-over, maybe a few stitches, then a couple of days in the barn would close the hole in her hip. But the hole in her heart, the loss of Bo, Mercie, and Rusty would never be healed.

Ken walked to where Rosco lay beside Gracie and Ginger. Looking down at the little dog, Ken marveled. He had come to Gateway as a scrawny runt, cast away in the midst of predators by one who had thought him worthless.

But he had survived the night. He had refused to allow the circumstances of the instant to define his future.

He had overlooked the betrayal of *one* to trust *the many* and had pushed through the limitations of life to achieve the goal he wanted most. To stand beside his peers, to be what he was designed to be and to reach his full potential as a member of the Gateway Posse.

Today he earned that membership. He faced and engaged in battle with those who sought to rule by fear, intimidation, and force.

He exacted justice for his little sister by standing up to those who had deprived her of her right to life.

He placed himself in harm's way to defend his home and his people, and in doing so, he overcame the fear that had haunted him since the hot August night so long ago.

He was now *Rosco Jack of Gateway Farm.*

# BOOK TWO

# ROSCO JACK & THE RETURN OF THE PIRATE

## The Storm

Collins lay still. He had chosen an elevated shelf of sediment deposited by the annual floods that turned the gently flowing stream into a raging torrent. The racing waters spilled out of the banks and swept over the landscape, dropping loose soil and other debris along the way. Here he was covered by the shadows created by the setting sun but still able to see any small animals approaching the water for a drink before they went into their dens for the night.

The air was still. That was both a blessing and a curse. The stillness prevented his scent from being carried to the wary animals approaching the stream, but it also prevented Collins from detecting their approach. He heard a movement through the fallen leaves and lifted his nose to try and catch the scent. Nothing. But there the sound was again; an animal was approaching the water.

Collins resisted the temptation to turn his head to look toward the sound. He saw movement out of the corner of his eye and felt his muscles tense for the charge. Then he saw it, a giant red squirrel.

Collins relaxed and released his held breath. The squirrel heard him exhale, jumped onto a tree, and scurried up to a limb extending out over the water. He looked Collins over and seemed to understand that he was not a threat.

Collins watched the squirrel clamber down the tree and prance down the slope to the creek. Collins watched him, remembering the day he and Rosco had tangled with another big red squirrel on Gateway Farm.

Both Collins and Rosco still carried the scars that sharp-toothed, bushy-tailed whirlwind inflicted on them.

*'Nope, I have no interest in tangling with another squirrel,'* Collins thought as the squirrel ignored him and drank his fill of the freshwater.

The stillness was ended by an icy blast of wind that swept down the little draw whistling through the giant oak trees lining the creek bank. He lifted his nose and sniffed the air. *'A storm is coming, and with it will come freezing rain,'* the scents told him.

Collins was hungry, but this was his second winter in the forest, and he had learned that his survival depended on remaining dry and protected from winter's fury.

He remembered seeing a higher spot further down the creek. An old oak had fallen during some long past storm and brush had sprung up around the downed giant.

He trotted that way now, thinking, '*Vines, which have trapped falling leaves, cover the brush. They will form a canopy under which I can find shelter. The creek will give me water, and I will hunt along its banks. Perfect,'* he thought as he increased his pace.

Collins found the spot and worked his way in under the dense canopy of vines, leaves, and brush. More leaves covered the ground. Collins scratched a nest out of the leaves and lay down with his back against the old tree.

Outside his den, the wind was now roaring along the creek carrying the smell of the coming rain. Collins moved to the opening and looked skyward. A wall of dark clouds was riding the wind in over the forest. A few raindrops splashed down, and Collins turned back from the opening and lay down again.

A flash of light illuminated his den, followed by a crash of thunder. The skies opened, and those few drops of rain became walls of water pushed through the forest by the north wind. Collins lifted his head and looked through the small opening of his lair. The creek was no longer visible; all he could see was the falling rain.

He dropped his head onto his paws and allowed his heavy eyelids to close. His last thought was, *'The temperature is dropping. This rain will turn to ice and then snow before morning.'* But Collins was protected from the storm, and he slept.

---

Hunger pangs woke Collins. He stood, stretched, and looked outside. Snow had fallen through the night and now clung to the vines covering the entrance. He could see that snow covered the ground. Collins pushed his way through the vines and lifted his nose to search for scents. He detected the ever-present squirrels, and rabbits. Collins trotted forward determined to find food.

Then he smelled a heavier scent. It was a deer. Collins stood frozen in his tracks. His ears were the only thing on him that moved. He turned them this way and then the other, but he could hear nothing but the sound of the wind whistling through the pine trees.

Collins sniffed again and smelled blood. He followed the scent, pushing through the deep snow and down the slope toward the creek. He rounded a bend in the creek bed and stopped. There in the snow was the remains of a fawn.

Collins could read the story in the blood-soaked snow. He circled the area sniffing the snow, and found the scent of the killer. It was a big cat. Collins could see the tracks of the cat as he left the scene after eating his fill of the little deer. He noticed that there were no tracks showing where the cat came in, just those of his leaving. Collins doubled back to the kill site and worked his way all around the body. Nothing, no sign of the cat stalking the deer.

Collins looked up and saw a large limb extending out from a pine over the spot where the fawn lay. '*The panther climbed the Pine and hid in the foliage, waiting. He dropped onto the deer from above. The weight of the panther took the fawn down, and the fight was short. Mom and the other deer ran for their lives, and the cat feasted on the fawn,*' Collins reasoned.

After making sure the cat had left the area, Collins ate his fill from the remains of the baby deer. Then he pulled the rest back to his lair, stopping from time to time, checking the scents and listening for any sign of the big cat. Collins did not want to tangle with a panther.

He pulled the deer into his den and pushed it into a corner. Then he trotted to the creek for a drink. He sat for a minute enjoying the warming sun as it peaked through the scattered clouds.

Energized by his meal, Collins ran along the creek exploring. He intended to spend the winter here and wanted to know what lay above and below his spot on the stream. He found a rabbit's den and checked to see if anyone was home. Finding none, he waded across a shallow part of the creek and raced up the bank. He stood on this high point and surveyed the area. The forest was quiet.

Collins crossed the creek and headed toward his den. He had just entered and laid down for a nap when he heard the approach of padded feet on the frozen snow. Collins moved to the opening and peeked out.

Standing there in the snow was the big cat. He had followed the smell of his kill right to the entrance of Collin's den.

Collins saw the anger in the cat's green eyes. The cat lowered his head and growled a warning to Collins.

Collins did not want to fight, but he was determined to defend his nest and the food that he would need to make it through this winter storm. He matched the cat's stare and growled back.

The cat took a couple of steps forward, and then to the side of the entrance. Collins could no longer see the cat, but he could hear him breathing and smell the heavy musk of the big male panther.

Collins knew the cat was trying to lure him outside. He also knew that his best chance to survive this encounter was by staying right where he was. To reach Collins, the cat would have to come in through the narrow opening, and Collins knew he could inflict serious injury on the intruder. The panther would have to expose his face and throat to Collins without being able to use his claws or size to his advantage.

The panther issued a screaming challenge. Collins stood his ground. The panther jumped onto the fallen tree and then walked across the top of the den. He was searching for a way in, but Collins knew there was only one way in: through the front opening.

The cat paced back and forth and then jumped down. He roared a second challenge for Collins to come out and fight. Collins ignored the taunt and watched as the big cat dropped to his belly and pushed his head through the vines. Collins struck.

He lunged forward, clamping his teeth down around the right side of the panther's face. Blood gushed into Collin's mouth as he bit down and shook while backing away from the entrance.

The panther screamed in pain and pulled free from Collins's grip. Collins could see blood streaming from the cat's mangled face.

The panther rolled, pushing the wound deep into the snow seeking to ease the pain. Then he was on his feet, charging forward again.

Collins waited until the cat had his head entirely inside the opening, then dropped to his belly and clamped down on the soft flesh of the cat's throat. He bit through the fur, and when he tasted blood, he ripped down and pulled back using all of his strength in one quick move.

The panther screamed again and backed out of the entrance. Collins could see the gaping wound. The cat had suffered a terrible injury, but it was not mortal. Collins realized that he had missed the big artery.

The pain and the loss of blood ended the fight for the panther. Collins watched as he disappeared into the woods. *'He will survive, but he will not be strong enough to attack me again this winter,'* Collins knew.

He waited a while to be sure the cat was gone and then laid down against his log. He was exhausted, and sleep came quickly. But before sleep claimed him, Collins decided, *'This is my last winter alone. In the spring, I am going back to Gateway Farm. I want to be a member of the posse if they will have me.'*

## Homeward Bound

Collins woke to the sound of water dripping off the roof of his den. He sniffed the air and detected a familiar smell. It was the smell of spring.

He stood, approached the opening and sniffed again, searching for any indication the big cat lay in wait outside his sanctuary. Once he was confident that no danger was present, he pushed through the wet vines and stretched his cramped muscles in the warming sun.

Collins made his way through the remaining patches of snow to the creek and drank deeply. Finished, he looked at his reflection in the water and saw that he had lost a lot of weight during his winter dormancy. *'I will gain back what I have lost once I reach Gateway. The Feeder will see to that,'* Collins thought as he remembered Mr. Ken bringing food to the Posse each morning.

Collins turned from the creek and started up the slope. He took one last look at his winter's home and then continued to the top of the little hill. As he reached the top, he stepped from the protected gully into a stiff breeze. The wind was out of the East and carried a chill. Collins shivered and was grateful for his thick mat of fur.

Collins knew that the way home lay in the East. He trotted forward, and a gust of wind struck him with a heavy musty smell. Collins stopped. He lifted his nose and examined the lingering scent.

It was the Panther. The hair on the back of his neck stood up, and a low growl started deep in his chest. Collins stood still. He was not going to turn away, *'I will have to face him sooner or later. Might as well be now,'* he thought.

He heard the soft padding of the Panther's pace and watched as the big cat rounded the corner in the path. The Panther saw Collins and stopped.

The two antagonists looked each other over. '*Those wounds are still partially open. His face and his mouth are swollen with infection. I bet he has real trouble eating. He has lost a lot of weight and looks weak. He poses no threat to me,*' Collins realized.

The cat tried to bare his teeth in a warning to Collins, but the pain of opening his mouth caused him to wince in pain. Collins lowered his head and advanced toward the cat in a stiff-legged march that said, *'don't mess with me.'*

The cat stepped aside. As Collins passed, the cat stretched his nose forward and sniffed him. Collins growled a warning, and the cat stepped back. Collins continued for a few steps and then stopped and watched as the Panther made his way down to the creek and drank his fill. Then the cat sat and dipped his paw into the cold water. He lifted the paw and tried to wash his injured face. Collins heard him cry out in pain as the clawed foot touched the open wound. He watched as the cat leaned forward, turned his head and dipped his wounded face into the creek. *'The cold water will numb the pain, and the gently flowing water will wash the infection out of the wound. He will stay here near the water, and wait for the wound to heal. That will take a while, and that means he will not be stalking me. But he took a deep smell of me. He is making sure that he has my scent so he can follow later. I have not seen the last of this big cat,'* Collins figured as he turned toward home.

---------------------------------------

Collins sat in the shade of the giant pines and looked across the pasture. East Texas was in the grips of an unusually hot and dry Spring. The drought and the heat now radiated up to dance in shimmering waves above the parched earth.

The tracking hounds of the prison across the way had caught his scent and were barking out their warning for him to stay out of their domain. Collins knew they were kenneled and did not pose any threat to him. He saw one of the guards come out of the tower and lift a pair of field glasses scanning the tree line in search of what had caught the hounds' attention.

Collins stood up and moved out of the shade into the sunlight so the officer could see him and know that there was no threat to the security of the prison. He watched the officer go back into the tower and knew that he would not be bothered by a patrol.

The brief time he spent in the sun caused Collins discomfort. He was a Great Pyrenees, and his thick matted long-haired winter coat caused him to suffer in the Texas heat. He could travel during the day if he had the shade of the Pine Forest to keep the sun off of him. Otherwise, he restricted his moved at night.

He stepped back into the deep shade and laid down again. A light breeze wafted through the trees, and Collins lifted his nose to sniff it. He smelled rain on the breeze and knew that the storm would hit before darkness fell.

He stretched out and allowed the past to flood his mind. He remembered Gateway Farm and the posse. His rebellion, his refusal to follow the rules of the posse, had led him to leave. He remembered hearing the master, Ken, tell Ms. Trudy, "Collins will not be here long. He is a rebel, a real pirate who insists on being the Captain of his fate and that attitude is going to result in much pain in his life."

Collins drifted into sleep and dreamed. He remembered sitting in the cab of his owner's truck and the man who opened the door and stole him. He whimpered, remembering the pain of being separated from his mother and littermates. The man had taken him to a house on the red dirt road across the way from where he now lay and used a rope to tie him to a post on the porch of the house.

The rope was just long enough to allow Collin to get off the porch to relieve himself. He lived tied up on that porch for three months. His growth had made the rope tighter and tighter around his neck and eventually began to choke him. His life was miserable.

Then the man opened the door one morning and stepped from the house carrying two suitcases. Collins watched as the man loaded the bags into his pickup and then turned back to the house. Collins wagged his tail as the man stepped up onto the porch. The man stopped and looked at Collins for a minute. Collins nosed his empty water dish hoping the man would fill it for him.

The man walked into the house and came out carrying two more cases. Collins heard more footsteps and looked to see the woman coming out of the house. She pulled the door closed, looked at Collins and said, "Jeff, what about this dog?"

"Get in the truck. The landlord will find him and cut him loose," Jeff replied.

"But he won't know we are gone for a week or more. That dog needs water and food. At least untie him and let him go," the woman said.

"Get in the truck, Mary. I want to get on the road. That dog will be okay," Jeff said.

Collins watched the truck until it was out of sight and then walked to the opposite end of the porch and laying down out of the hot sun. The day grew hotter, as the sun rose higher in the sky and Collins thirst was now raging.

Late in the afternoon, a summer shower popped up, and Collins drank rainwater from where it collected in a muddy puddle at the corner of the house. He was still hungry, but the rain brought relief from the searing heat and enabled him to appease his thirst.

The next two days passed in much the same way, except there were no more rain showers. By the end of the third day, Collins was desperate. He knew that he had to find food and water or he would die on the porch.

Collins lay down and started chewing on the rope. His dry mouth was soon bleeding from the constant irritation of the rough rope. He stopped for a while and then started chewing again. He finally chewed through the rope.

He was weak from dehydration and hunger. He stood and stepped onto the first step leading off the porch. His weak legs collapsed, and he rolled into the yard.

Collins pushed himself to his feet and staggered to the ditch where the long grass and weeds were coated with the morning dew. He lay in the ditch licking the grass until the moisture began to cool his tongue.

He stood once more, knowing that he had to find water.

The rope was still tied around his neck, and a length of it trailed behind him, catching on roots and rocks. The effort to pull free was more than he could manage, and he lay down again.

Collins was drifting into unconsciousness when he felt the vibrations of a vehicle coming down the road. He was laying in the road and knew that he might be hit, but he could not garner the strength to move out of the way.

Collins heard the truck stop and then the sound of footsteps approaching him. He listened to the soothing voice of a man who Collins knew cared about him. The man kneeled beside Collins, removed the rope from around his neck and gently lifted him out of the road.

He carried Collins to his truck and laid him in the bed. Collins felt the truck began to move, and then he passed out.

When he woke, Collins heard the man's voice again. Collins smelled water. He sat up and saw that the man had placed a bowl of water in front of where he had slept. Collins lapped it up and then saw the man putting another bowl filled with milk in front of him. Collins drank the last drop and then licked the bowl.

He looked up and saw that four other dogs were approaching. They smelled him and then laid down, signaling that he was accepted.

A bolt of lightning flashed across the sky, and the following explosion of thunder woke Collins from his dreams. He sat up and watched as a curtain of rain advanced across the pasture toward the trees where he sat.

The rain washed over him, and he stood, allowing it to soak through to his hot skin. Collins held still until the cooling rain had lowered his core temperature. Then he trotted across the pasture, making sure he splashed through every puddle. He paused at the edge of the red dirt road and then turned toward Gateway Farm. The Pirate was returning; Collins was heading home.

## The Aftermath

Collins trotted down the middle of the road. The wet, cool mud felt good to his sore feet. He lifted his head and sniffed the air. There, riding on the dampness, was a familiar smell. Gateway Farm.

Collins rounded the curve in the road and paused. There in front of him was the house where he had been left tied to the porch. Collins remembered returning to that house to visit with the new residents, and in passing by the night, he decided to leave the farm.

He moved on, and soon the green iron gates of Gateway Farm came into sight. The gates were open, and the wet asphalt drive was shimmering in the sun. It was just as he remembered.

Collins started walking toward those open gates. He felt his heart lurch as he passed through them, and then he was running. He loped past the house where Ms. Flo lived and saw the big red barn. He stopped and took it all in.

There was the garden where he had lain while Mr. Roy and the Breaking Free guys planted. Beyond the garden, he could see the little pond where Mr. Ken had released Big Blue after their battle. And then he saw Rosco.

Rosco was laying on the drive in front of the barn. Collins could tell that he had changed. No longer was he the little puppy that ran the woods with Collins. There was something about he held his head; what was it?

Rosco caught the scent of Collins and stood to face him. He lifted his nose and breathed deeply, and then his tail began to wag. Collins looked at Rosco standing tall and thought, *'He is standing with a confidence he did not have before. He has become a member of the posse, and Rosco has grown up.'*

Rosco took a step forward and woofed. Collins felt his tail begin to wag in reply to the greeting. He saw movement from within the shadows of the barn, and there came Gracie, followed by Ginger.

Ginger strode to the end of the drive and stood with her head lowered and eyes fixed on Collins. Gracie and Collins stood beside her. Collins recognized the challenge. Ginger's posture said it all. *'So, the Pirate has returned. To stay, you must first submit yourself to me and agree to follow the rules of the posse. We are one. We act as one, and we acknowledge that our first duty is to the protection of this farm and its' inhabitants.'*

Collins approached Ginger slowly and lay down in front of her. He rolled over onto his back and remained still as she stood over him. Ginger sniffed him and then stepped back. Rosco and Gracie were next. They each smelled him and then sat down beside Ginger. Collins knew that they were saying to Ginger, 'We *accept him, but the decision is yours.'*

Ginger walked over and licked Collin in his face. His heart jumped as he realized that she was giving him a second chance. He rolled from his back onto his feet and began to run in a circle, barking out his joy.

The posse sat watching him. He stopped in front of them and touched noses with each one. *'Thank you'* was in his heart.

Ginger turned to find a place to lie in the shade. It was then that Collins noticed the wound on her side. He looked at Gracie and saw scars on her also, and Rosco was limping as if he was sore and stiff. *'They have been in a war,'* he realized.

Collins looked around for Bo and Mercie. He walked over to Rosco and nosed him asking, *'What happened? Where is Bo? Where are Mercie and Rusty?'*

Collins nosed Rosco again and caught the scent of the big cats. Turning, he walked to Gracie and then to Ginger. He sniffed deeply at the wound in her side, and there it was again, the smell of the big cat.

Collins trotted over to Rosco and lay down beside him. Rosco rolled over to rest against Collins and sighed. Collins turned his head to lick Rosco and saw five mounds of dark earth piled beside the barn. He trotted over and sniffed. *'There is Gracie; Bo is under this dirt, Rusty lies here, and the big cats are there.'*

Rosco came up beside him and whined in his sorrow. Collins could guess it all. The showdown with the big cats had come. It had been a battle in which the Posse opposed the big cats' effort to dominate the residents of Gateway Farm.

Collins could smell the gunpowder working its' way through the soil where one of the cats lay and knew that Mr. Ken had been there. But the battle had been borne by the posse. They had defended the residents of the farm, and in doing so, three had given their lives. Collins sighed, *'Freedom is not free.'*

## The First Patrol

Collins heard the deep breathing and realized that the exhausted Posse members had surrendered to their bodies' demands. Wounds and stressed muscles had pulled them into a coma-like sleep. He glanced at the sky and saw that no more than two hours of sunlight remained. *'Let them rest,'* he thought, lying beside Rosco.

---

Ginger woke first. She looked to the west and saw that the sun was dropping quickly. Soon it would be below the horizon, and darkness would cover the farm. She stood and nosed Gracie awake. Then she woke Collins and Rosco.

She looked over her posse. The absence of Rusty, Bo, and Mercie stood out to her. Collins was a big dog. He was healthy and young but not ready to replace the larger and more experienced Rusty and Bo. And Mercie, the lion-hearted one, was gone. Gracie was next to her in seniority, and Rosco was willing but so small.

She wagged her tail to reassure her deputies and stepped out in a trot. She wanted to patrol the boundaries of the farm before full darkness settled in.

Ginger led the posse to the front gate and then turned east to run along the dirt road bordering the farm, then back to the south to follow the fence through the forest, down past the little pond, and into the lower pasture. She paused there, disturbed by the heavy scent of wild hogs.

They crossed the damn between the smaller and larger pond and into the pasture beyond. The horses lifted their heads to watch the patrol and then returned to grazing, confident that these were protectors, not predators.

Here the smell of the hogs was even stronger, and Ginger could see where they had rooted up the ground to feed on the tender roots. They had cut a swath across the pasture, leaving holes and trenches that made it difficult to cross on foot and almost impossible for Mr. Roy and Mr. Ken to work the land with their tractors. *'We are going to have to deal with these hogs. But how? Collins is inexperienced, Rosco and Gracie are too small, and my wound prevents me from engaging in full combat,'* she thought.

She led on, and the posse turned back toward Mr. Ken and Ms. Trudy's house. As they dropped down into a draw behind the damn, Ginger smelled a Bobcat. She followed the scent trail and found him hiding in some blackberry vines along the back of the damn. She recognized his scent and knew that he came each night at this time to drink from the ponds. The cat sat still and watched Ginger as she sniffed the air. He eyed the posse nervously but was confident that Ginger would leave him alone.

Ginger turned away and ran toward the upper pasture to check out the cattle shed. As she approached, she detected the odor of a snake. Ginger knew that some snakes were harmless and that Mr. Ken liked them because they helped control the big field rats that chewed up the wiring in the barns and ate the grain he had stored up for his animals. But this was not one of those.

Ginger stopped. Rosco and Gracie stood beside her, waiting for her instructions. But Collins had trotted on ahead. Ginger realized that he had not picked up the scent of the snake yet. She barked a warning, and Collings turned back to her.

She scouted ahead of the posse, checking the ground for the scent trail of the serpent. She crossed it in front of the opening to the cattle shelter.

*'That is a Timber Rattler, and from the size of the trail, this is going to be a big one,'* Ginger reasoned.

She moved back from the scent trail, checking the grass on each side of the little path leading into the shelter. *'These snakes like to lie alongside a pathway and wait for prey. They will strike quickly, inject large amounts of their deadly venom and then wait for the victim to die before consuming it. But the danger lies in their being so aggressive that they will strike anything moving along that pathway. That makes them dangerous to our people and the other animals here on the farm. We have to find him and either convince him to return to the forest or kill him. There are no other options,'* she reasoned.

The posse waited as Ginger checked along the pathway. She looked at them and then turned back toward the shelter. She knew they would follow in her steps. As they approached the entrance, Ginger heard the serpent slide through the grass, and then she saw him. *'There he is,'* Ginger thought.

The snake coiled and raised his tail, shaking it to make the rattles on the end sound.

Ginger saw his head and watched as he flicked his tongue in and out. *'We are too far away for him to strike, but he is ready should we come closer. He will not leave; this is going to be a fight to the death,'* Ginger knew.

Collins and Rosco moved up to stand on Ginger's left side, and Gracie moved up even with her on the right. The serpent moved his head back and forth, measuring the distance and preparing for the fight.

*'I need him to strike while we are still out of range, but how do I get him to do that,'* Ginger wondered.

She lowered her head to protect her throat and stepped forward. The snake fixed his eyes on her.

Ginger feinted as if she was going to jump forward, but instead, she moved quickly to the right pushing Gracie aside. The serpent launched out with fangs bared but found only air where Ginger had been.

Ginger turned her head while in mid-air and clamped down behind the head of the serpent. She bit down and felt her teeth cut through the muscle and into cartilage. She whipped her head back and forth to break the snake's spine, but he was too strong and full of fight.

The snake wrapped its' lower body around Ginger's neck and started to squeeze. At the same time, he was trying to break her grasp on his head. Ginger knew that if he were able to get his head free while wrapped around her neck, he would be able to strike her repeatedly in the face. She had to break his hold on her neck.

Ginger bit down harder and started to move her teeth back and forth in a sawing motion. The snake released his hold in response to the pain, and Ginger flung him against the wall of the cattle shelter.

The snake was dazed. Gracie dashed in, grabbed him by the tail, and swung him against the wall again. Collins sprung forward and placed both paws on the snake's back, just behind his head. He then leaned forward, using all of his weight to pin the snake securely against the ground.

Rosco ran forward and locked his teeth into the wound left by Ginger's initial attack. He bit down and felt the cartilage part. He bit harder and ripped back and out. The bone broke, and the snake's head separated from his body. Rosco tossed it aside and stepped back.

The snake's body continued to move, writhing in the grass. Ginger knew it posed no danger, but she also knew the head could still bite and inject venom. She stepped forward and looked at the serpent. His eyes were still open and focused on her. As she got closer, the snake's mouth opened, and the fangs were extended. Ginger watched as the venom dripped from them, knowing the snake was not yet dead and still full of fight.

She stepped back and sat down. The posse followed her and sat beside her to wait. The snake died as darkness fell. Ginger checked to ensure this threat to the farm had been removed and then led the posse toward the houses.

As the patrol circled the last house and headed toward the barn, Ginger looked toward the tree line and saw movement.

She paused and lifted her nose to test for a scent. The hair on her back stood up, and a growl escaped as she recognized the smell of a panther.

Collins stepped forward and sniffed deeply. The wind brought the scent to him, and he recognized the odor of the panther from the creek. His head lowered, and he took a couple of steps forward.

Ginger snapped at him, and he fell back. She looked at the tree line and saw the moonlight bouncing off of the eyes of the big cat.

She turned toward the barn, and the posse fell in behind her. The cat issued a roaring challenge, but the posse ignored him. *'Soon, we will deal with you. But not tonight, not in the darkness. We will dictate the when and where,'* Ginger reasoned and padded on toward her bed and a nap.

The posse would patrol again at midnight, and she needed her rest. She looked at Collins and thought, *'He did well on his first patrol. The posse is stronger with him as a member. Welcome home, Collins.'*

## The Masked Bandit

The moon was full and high in the sky when Ginger woke at midnight. She stood, stretched her sore muscles, and moved out of the barn into the darkness on the side, away from the moon. She waited while the posse gathered alongside her and then trotted across the garden toward the fence that ran down the east side of the farm. Here the massive oaks blotted out the moon's light, offering the posse a protective covering from prying eyes.

Ginger slowed the pace to a walk. She kept her eyes on the ground, taking care to avoid stepping on anything that would signal their passage. She wanted to check the perimeter, to see without being seen.

The Posse followed her, one behind the other. Each deputy had sensed her desire for stealth.

Ginger led on, watching the ground and using her keen sense of smell to check for scents of danger. She found nothing but the usual night-time visitors along the fence line and turned toward the ponds.

She led the patrol across the pastures, past the still body of the serpent, and turned toward the houses. As she approached Mr. Ken and Ms. Trudy's house, she picked up a familiar scent. Her ears perked up, and a soft growl grew in her chest. *'That smells like Ralph, and Ralph always means trouble,'* Ginger thought as she broke into a lope.

She raced past the front porch, following the scent trail toward the back of the house. She heard the springs on the porch gate squeak as it opened.

*'That is Ralph! He just pushed through the gate, and I can hear him pulling the lid off of the bin where Mr. Ken keeps our food. That bandit is stealing from us again,'* Ginger was in a full run, barking as she rounded the corner.

Collins slid around the corner right behind Ginger. She ran up the steps, and Collins followed her. The gate at the top of the steps was now closed, blocking their access to the porch. Ginger tried to jump the barrier, but it was too high. She rested her front paws on top of the gate, and Collins followed suit.

Ginger was staring toward the darkest corner of the porch, and Collins leaned forward to see what had captured her attention. As he watched, the fattest raccoon Collins had ever seen crawled out of a grey storage bin, glanced at Ginger and sat on his haunches chewing on the food he had taken from the container.

Collins sniffed the air and caught the odor of the chunky nuggets that Mr. Ken fed them. He narrowed his eyes and could see that the raccoon was holding a nugget between his two front paws and nibbling on it while watching Ginger and the Posse. *'He seems to be smiling at us, more of a smirk, really,'* Collins thought.

The house's back door opened, and Collins saw Mr. Ken coming out with a flashlight in one hand and a pistol in the other. Ginger saw him at the same time.

She turned, ran down the steps, and led the Posse away from the porch, but Collins remained by the gate. He heard a scratching noise and turned to see the raccoon climb up a post and jump onto the roof of the house. Mr. Ken heard it too.

Collins joined the Posse and watched as Mr. Ken walked down the steps and turned to look toward the roof of the house. He lifted the flashlight and searched along the roof with the beam of light. The light moved slowly across the lower level of the roof, and then Mr. Ken moved it higher. And, there sat the raccoon, smack in the middle of the beam of light.

Collins heard Mr. Ken say, "Well, well. Hello, there Ralph. What in the world are you doing sitting on my roof at this time of night?"

Ralph finished chewing his last piece of food and dropped his front paws onto the roof. He wrapped his tail around his feet and yawned.

"Bored are you, Ralph?" Mr. Ken said. Collins looked again at Ralph and was surprised to see that the bandit had laid down and was now snoring lightly.

Collins watched as Mr. Ken walked over to where Ginger was sitting. He pushed the pistol inside his belt, bent over, and rubbed Ginger's head, saying, "Good job Ginger. You caught that bandit red-handed.

I could shoot him off of the house, but I won't. I am going to go back inside and get into my warm, soft bed. You and the Posse keep Ralph on the roof. He won't be sleeping so soundly as the temperature drops, and he gets tired of that hard roof. I'll come back out here when the sun is up and make a decision on what to do with that masked bandit."

Ginger wagged her tail as Mr. Ken climbed the steps and went back into the house.

Then she moved among the Posse, sniffing each one. Rosco and Gracie lay down and went to sleep. Ginger sat down, focused on the roof, then turned to Collins and whined.

Collins moved up beside her, and Ginger lay down to sleep. Collins realized she wanted him to stand the first watch, keeping the raccoon Mr. Ken had called Ralph on the roof. He sat on his haunches and focused his attention on the dark spot at the top of the roof that he knew was Ralph.

---

Collins was sleeping when he heard the door to the house open. He sat up and watched as Mr. Ken came walking down the steps. All of the Posse was up now, and Mr. Ken said, "Good morning, boys and girls. Let's see what Ralph is up to this morning."

He turned and lifted his hand to shade the morning sun from his eyes and called out, "Well, good morning, you Ole Masked Bandit. I bet you are ready to get off of that roof. Not the most comfortable place to spend the night, is it?"

Collins glanced at Ginger and saw that her ears were up, and he could hear a growl coming from deep in her chest. He looked at the roof and saw that Ralph did indeed look ready to get down from that roof. He was pacing back and forth, working his way down from the top to the lowest part, above where the gutters were attached.

Ralph looked at Mr. Ken and then at the Posse. *'It looks as if he is asking Mr. Ken to call us off, to let him get down and escape into the woods,'* Collins thought.

"Yep, just as I thought. You now realize that nothing is free. Stealing, and that is what you were doing; you bandit. And stealing always ends up costing you more than you are willing to pay.

I know you want me to call the Posse off so you can get down, but I'm not sure you have learned your lesson, Ralph. I will leave them here for a while longer and let you think about the cost of your lazy, thieving ways.

I will be back about noon. By then, you will have learned your lesson. If I see that your attitude has changed, then I will let you down, and you can run off into the woods.

But if not, well, I might turn you into a cap to keep my head warm this winter. Watch him, Ginger, hold him up there, and I will bring breakfast to you and your deputies," Mr. Ken said and turned back to the house.

Collins looked at Ralph and felt a bit of sympathy for him. '*I hope he does get his attitude right. I don't want to see Mr. Ken shoot him; he needs to get back into the woods and stay there. But if he doesn't if he continues his thieving ways, then we will do our duty,*' Collins mused as he lay down with his focus on Ralph.

## Death Watches

The cool air of the morning had long since passed. Now the mid-day sun beat down, and the heat was unbearable for Collins. His thick coat hung on him like a heavy blanket, robbing him of energy and leaving him unable to pull his fair share of standing watch over Ralph.

He lay in the shade of the house as Ginger paced back and forth, glancing now and then at the roof where Ralph was suffering even more than Collins. Rosco and Gracie lay near Collins, waiting their turn to relieve Ginger in keeping the watch.

Mr. Ken stepped out of the barn and looked toward the house. He could see the Posse laying in the shade provided by the roof overhang while Ginger stood watch, keeping Ralph on top of the house. Ken shaded his eyes and looked at the sun which was straight overhead now. *"Noon, time to call the Posse off and let Ralph come down,"* he said to himself.

Ken picked up two of the metal bowls he used to feed the Posse, and began to bang one against the other. He could see that the Posse had heard the clanging and was up and running for the barn.

Ken watched as Ralph made his way down from the roof and ran for the cool shade of the forest. Suddenly, Ralph turned away from the tree line and came running toward the barn.

"Now, what is that about?" Ken muttered.

Ralph stopped short of the barn and sat looking at Ken. Ken could tell that the heat had sapped Ralph's strength and that the once-sassy raccoon was near exhaustion. His heart would not allow Ken to watch Ralph's suffering any longer.

He picked up the water hose, ran a bowl full, and sat it in the shade for Ralph. Ken stepped back from the pan and watched to see if Ralph would trust him enough to drink.

Thirst was driving Ralph to forgo his natural distrust of man, but still, he hesitated. He eyed Ken and reasoned that the man was standing far enough away from the water that escape would be possible should he exhibit any hostile intent.

Ralph lifted his nose and sniffed. He smelled the water, and its' promise of life pushed his fear aside. Ralph moved closer while watching Ken. Reaching the bowl, he bent to lap a few mouthfuls and then sat up to see what Ken was up doing.

*'He is just watching. I don't see anything in his stance to indicate he intends to harm me,'* Ralph reasoned.

He dropped his head into the bowl and drank his fill. Finished, he looked up and saw that Ken was gone. But he had left another bowl, and this one held dog food.

Ralph was hungry and moved quickly to the unexpected treat. As he chewed, Ralph thought about how things had changed. *'Last night, he put the Posse after me, but today he feeds me. Why?'* Ralph asked himself.

The sound of movement put Ralph on the alert. He ran to the edge of the shade and waited. Ginger and the rest of the Posse came around the corner, and the man was with them.

Ralph started to run, but where would he go? He looked nervously at the tree line and then back at Ken.

Ken saw Ralph's hesitation and followed his glance toward the trees. "What is it, Ralph? What is keeping you from escaping into the forest?" Ken asked.

Ginger and the Posse lay at Ken's feet, watching Ralph. Ginger had recognized the change in circumstances and waited for her master's instruction. The Posse waited on her.

"Come on, Ginger," Ken said and stepped out of the shade, walking toward the trees. Ginger led the Posse along behind Ken, and Ralph followed the Posse.

As they neared the trees, Ken pointed to toward them and said, "Check it, Ginger."

Ginger raced forward with her Posse following. Ginger lifted her nose and sniffed. As she did, the scream of a big cat echoed across the farm.

"Come back here, Ginger," Ken shouted.

Ginger turned and trotted back to sit beside her master. Ken rubbed her head and said, "Good girl. Now we know why Ralph would not go into the forest. There is a panther in there. He is a predator and considers every living thing on the Farm as his prey."

Ken turned to look at Ralph and saw that the fat bandit was running full tilt for the safety of the barn. He watched as Ralph ran into the stall area of the barn and, without slowing, climbed into the hayloft.

Ken laughed, "I understand your fear, but Ralph, my friend, that loft will not provide you protection from this panther. He will leap easily into your lair.

No, as long as he is here, no living thing is safe. So, I will encourage him to move on, and if he doesn't, well, we will do what we must," Ken said.

---

The big cat lay behind a fallen tree and watched the man and the dogs at the edge of the tree line. He had seen the big white dog. He didn't need the scent to know that this was the one he had come to kill.

He had screamed out the warning because he was still weak, and the wounds from their last battle needed more time to heal. He had not been able to eat because of the injuries to his jaw. Hunger pangs were now his constant companion.

The wounds on his face were itching as they healed. He lifted his paw and rubbed it gently across his face to relieve the itch. The sharp pain caused him to whimper, and he saw that the dogs had heard him.

He watched their leader and saw her ears perk up and point directly to where he lay. He knew she could not see him, but her hearing and sense of smell enabled her to know where he was.

The big white dog growled and moved forward. The cat thought he was coming in, but the leader blocked his way and turned him back to sit with the others.

*'I will need to take her out first. Without their leader, the others will be easy to kill. I will save the big white one for last. I will make him suffer as he has me. But for now, I need to find a place to rest and grow strong again,'* the cat thought as he rose and moved into the forest.

He paused for one last look at his enemy. They were following the man back toward the barn, but they kept glancing back warily at the forest. *'They know that death was watching them. They know that a battle is coming,'* he thought as he padded softly across the forest floor.

## The Lesson

Ginger was unsettled. She paced back and forth, trying to formulate a plan for dealing with the panther. She paused and looked at the posse. They were laying in the shade, but every eye focused on her.

One by one, she examined her deputies. *'Rosco and Gracie are battle tested. They will be in the fight until the end. Collins did well against the serpent. I can count on him; his size will be important to us in this fight.*

*I will send Rosco in first. He is small and quick enough to torment the panther by darting in for a quick nip and then retreating out of his reach.*

*Once Rosco has distracted the panther, I will send Gracie in. She will jump on his back, grab a mouthful of his skin at the nape of his neck and hold on.*

*The panther will whirl in circles trying to dislodge Gracie. He will also turn his head, trying to reach and bite her. He will be off balance and desperate to get her off his back.*

*I will send Collins charging into him. The impact will knock him off of his feet, and he will turn his head to bite his tormentor.*

*I will be right behind Collins and watch for the cat's throat to be exposed; then, I will end it.*

*But, we must search and destroy him before he regains his strength. If not, he will kill or inflict serious injuries on my posse.*

*We leave at first light. I know where he is, and this must be settled now.*

Her plan was complete; Ginger lay down and slept.

---

Ginger woke suddenly. Something had changed; she could feel it. She lay still and allowed her senses to search the darkness of the barn. She found nothing that posed a threat.

A gust of wind swept through the open barn door bearing the scent of rain. Ginger stood and sniffed the air. The wind was blowing harder now, whistling through the barn and carrying the first drops of rain from the leading edge of the coming storm.

A flash of light lit up the interior of the barn. It was followed by a clap of thunder that shook the ground. Ginger heard Gracie whine and turned to look at her. She knew that Gracie was terrified of thunder. Ginger moved closer to Gracie and nuzzled her softly.

The rest of the posse was awake now, and Ginger led them deeper into the barn, away from the open door. The first drops of rain splattered on the tin roof, and then the storm broke.

Ginger recognized the sound of hailstones as they pounded down on the roof. The wind was blowing so hard that the rain and hail were falling in horizontal sheets, slamming into the sides of the barn like battering rams.

Ginger snuggled deeper into the straw covering the barn's floor. Her last thought before sleep robbed her of consciousness was, *'This rain will wash away any tracks the panther may have left. But, I know where he is.'*

The sun rose over a water-logged gateway farm. Ginger moved the posse out to the feeding area and made them wait for Mr. Ken to bring their breakfast. She wanted each deputy to have a full stomach. She would lead them miles into the forest, and the route she would take was not easy.

Ginger sat patiently, waiting on Gracie to finish her bowl of food. Gracie ate very slowly and was always the last to finish. Finally, Gracie looked up, ran her tongue around the outside of her snout, and strolled over for a drink of water.

Ralph had been watching as each dog finished their meal. He inspected the bowl to see if there were any leftovers for him. He scored with Gracie's dish and was busy eating what she had left as Ginger led the posse across the front pasture and into the forest.

The dripping leaves and rivulets of water running across the wet forest floor soaked the posse from head to toe within minutes. Ginger led the posse directly to the fallen tree behind which the big cat had lain yesterday.

She circled the tree looking for tracks and sniffing the ground for any scent trail that might give her a clue as to the direction the cat had taken. There were none. She raised her head, looked around to orient herself, and then led her deputies out in a trot toward the lair where she believed this panther might be holed up.

A half-hour later, the posse could hear the roar of rushing water. Ginger slowed them to a walk and approached the creek that generally ran just inches deep and a few feet wide. But now it was swollen by the night's rain and had overflowed its banks. It was rushing through the forest with a force that would sweep the dogs off their feet and push them downstream, bouncing off stumps, stones and through little whitewater rapids.

Ginger remembered a spot around the bend to her right where a giant oak tree had fallen across the streambed. She led the posse in that direction, hoping it was still there, and as she rounded the bend, she could see that the tree was there and that it stretched all the way across the flooded stream.

She approached the site slowly and saw that the overflow had reached out to surround the base of the fallen tree. She stepped into the water and waded toward the tree. The pooling water was flowing gently here, but the closer she got to the tree, the deeper the water became. It was lapping against her belly when she reached the tree.

Ginger climbed onto the trunk and looked back at the posse. She knew that Gracie and Collins could wade to the tree, but Rosco would have to swim. She jumped from the downed tree and splashed through the rising water to where the posse sat waiting. She nudged Collins and Gracie forward, and they stepped into the water and made their way to the tree. Ginger waited until they had climbed out of the water and then turned to Rosco.

She stepped into the water and looked back at Rosco. He followed her and, within a few steps, was swimming. Ginger stayed beside him to ensure that the current did not sweep him into the rushing stream. As he reached the tree bridge, she placed her snout under him and gently lifted him until his front paws could gain traction on the rough bark of the downed tree. He pulled himself up and shook the water from his coat.

Ginger jumped onto the tree and led her deputies across the rushing water and onto the soggy ground beyond. She turned back to her left and loped toward the big cat's lair.

She remembered that it was a cave in the bank of a stream three times the size of the one they had just crossed. The posse would have to cross that water barrier, and there were no tree bridges to give them passage.

She also remembered that the opening of the cave was small. To enter, the deputies would have to drop to their bellies and crawl in one at a time. Ginger knew that they would be unable to defend themselves, and the cat would kill them quickly. *'Maybe the storm waters flooded the cave. If we can catch him in the open, we will have a chance,'* she thought as she led the posse on in search of this one who posed such a threat to the Farm.

An hour later, Ginger changed from a lope to a trot and looked back to check on her deputies. She could tell they needed a rest and stopped on a rise in a clearing filled with the bright sunshine of noon. A quick wind was sweeping through the forest, drying the ground and providing relief from the constant dripping.

Ginger knew they were close to the lair. She decided to let her deputies rest before leading them into danger. She lay down, and the posse followed suit.

Ginger stretched out and was quickly asleep. But even as she slept, her senses remained alert. And it was her sense of smell that woke her.

She sat up with an involuntary growl growing in her chest. She lifted her nose and sniffed. *'That is the cat, and he is close,'* she knew.

She glanced at the posse and saw that they were awake and had detected the scent too. She stood and followed the scent cones as they drifted overhead, borne by the southerly breeze.

The smell was growing stronger, and now Ginger could hear the sound of the rushing stream.

She looked back, and the posse responded by coming alongside her. She now led her little force forward in battle array expecting to see their adversary at any minute. Ginger slowed the pace to a walk. The passage of the wind through the trees was creating enough of a noise to keep her from hearing any movement of her prey, but she could now smell the musky odor of the wet cat strongly enough to know that he no more than a few feet from them.

She stopped the advance and started checking the forest in front of her, moving her eyes slowly from one section to the next. She saw a tangle of briars and brush off to the left and knew that he was there.

Ginger dropped her head and growled softly. The posse closed ranks, each dog moving together until they were shoulder to shoulder.

They moved forward as one, each concentrating on one dark mass within the briars. Ginger stopped the advance as that dark mass moved, then came out of the briars. The big cat stood with his head held high as if in disdain of the posse posing any threat to his unprotected throat.

Ginger could see that the big cat was still weak from the wounds inflicted on him by Collins. He was also wet, and his movements were sluggish, suggesting to her that the storm had flushed him out of his cave and that it had been necessary for him to swim the flood and then climb the high-cut bank to reach safety.

*'He is bluffing. Escaping the flood has taken a toll on him. He is in no shape to fight. He is hoping that we will leave him, as we did yesterday. Sorry, big fella, but no can do. This ends now.*

*I will not leave you to grow strong and become a threat to the Farm. You can turn and run, leaving this forest forever. Or we will kill you here and now. Let's see what your decision is,'* Ginger thought.

Collins stepped forward, out of line, and Ginger nipped him on the shoulder. Accepting her discipline, he stepped back so the panther faced a solid wall of bared teeth once more.

Ginger looked to her left at Gracie and then back to the cat. Gracie knew to move forward and stop. Ginger then looked to her right at Collins, who moved forward and stopped.

Rosco stepped out in front of Ginger so that now the posse faced the cat in a cup-shaped formation. Satisfied, Ginger nosed Rosco ahead, and the line moved in on the cat.

The panther dropped his head, covering his throat, and issued a warning scream. He rocked from one side to the other, sizing his enemies up. The big white dog was on his left. That was the one that the cat wanted, but if he broke that way, his right flank would be exposed.

The posse closed in on the cat, and he dropped to his belly. Ginger halted the advance. *'He has reduced his ability to move quickly, but he has also presented us with a more difficult target. If we rush him, he will spring up, ripping our bellies and throats. I have to get him to stand up,'* she thought.

She nudged Rosco, and he exploded forward, racing straight at the panther's nose. The suddenness of the charge by the little dog surprised the cat. He reacted slowly, allowing Rosco to dart in and rip a strip of flesh from the tender nostrils and then dodge the sweeping crush of the cat's big paw.

Blood pulsed up from the wound and filled the right eye of the panther, blinding him temporarily.

That was all Ginger needed. She led the charge, and the posse struck hard. Collins hit the panther shoulder high and rolled him over onto his back. Gracie grabbed a mouth full of the loose skin on the back of his head and jerked up and back.

The cat turned his head to deal with this searing pain, and Ginger took the left side of his face in her mouth and bit down, crushing the orbital socket in which the left eye rested. The eyeball popped out and hung by a bloody strip of flesh.

Rosco raced forward, grabbed the hanging eyeball, and ripped it off. He flung the bloody mess aside and stepped back once again, avoiding the massive paw.

The cat rolled onto his feet and turned, facing away from the pain inflicted by his tormentors. Maimed and blinded by pain, the cat staggered away from the fight. Ginger held the posse in check and watched him go.

He turned and moved toward his lair, and Ginger led the posse after him at a walk. He reached the water's edge and stopped. He knew he was not strong enough to swim that racing flood. His escape was blocked.

He faced the posse and waited for their charge. He did not issue a warning scream. He knew it was over.

Ginger kept the posse in check. She stared at her enemy and decided, '*There is no need to kill him. He is finished. He will never pose a threat to the Farm again.*'

She sat and then lay on the ground in front of the cat. The posse lay beside her.

The panther knew she was offering him a chance at life. He moved away along the bank of the stream without looking back. He was weak and needed a place to heal. He would leave this forest and never return.

His mind was made up; the big cat moved forward with a stronger step. He had learned a valuable lesson. No matter how big one is, you can push others only so far before they turn and fight. For the rest of his life he would respect the right of others to live free of fear.

He never again wanted to face an enemy as formidable as the Gateway Posse.

---

Collins lay with the posse watching the panther's retreat. He whined and inched forward, wanting to pursue his enemy.

A low growl issued from Ginger, and Collins moved back to lay beside her. He watched as she lay her head on her outstretched paws. He knew that this signaled her intent to let the panther go.

Rosco trotted over and licked his face. Then he lay across Collins outstretched paws as if to say, 'Let *it go, Collins.*'

Later, Ginger led the posse back toward the farm, and Collins found himself watching her. They crossed paths with rabbits and squirrels and came up on a big timber rattler crawling across their path. The snake was exactly like the one that they had killed his first night on the farm. But this time, Ginger stopped and let the serpent go in peace.

Once the snake had disappeared into the leaves, Ginger glanced at Collins and then moved the posse forward toward home. Collins came to realize that she was making a statement.

He thought, '*She is saying that we killed the rattler on the farm because he came to prey on the inhabitants of Gateway. But out here in the forest, the snake posed no threat to the Farm, so we left him alone.*

*We do that which is necessary to protect those we are responsible for. But we do not use our strength to impose our will, our way of life on others. We are a force; a posse, to keep the peace, to protect, and to serve. And I am a full member of the Gateway Posse. The Pirate is home!*'

**The End**

## About The Author

When asked at age ten what he most wanted the Lord to do for him, Ken responded, "*to give me a family and to allow me to be a police officer, a guardian of the peace.*" The Lord heard Ken that day and graced him with a wonderful wife, Trudy Turner Bangs, two wonderful children, and now two *perfect* grandchildren.

He began his career in law enforcement and public safety walking a beat in downtown Dallas at age nineteen. He retired after serving thirty-five years the last twenty-five as the director of police, security and student safety services for the Plano Independent School District.

After retirement, Ken and Trudy moved to Gateway Farm, where they lived for the next ten years. During their time at Gateway Farm they operated a home for children in the care of Child Protective Services.

An ordained minister, Ken also served as the senior pastor for Regions Christian Center in Texarkana, Texas.

Ken earned a B.S. in Criminal Justice from Sam Houston State University, a M.S. in Human Relations and Business Management from Amber University and a Doctorate of Ministry in Christian Counseling from Jacksonville Theology Seminary.

Ken and Trudy have been married 54 years and now live in McKinney, Texas.

An aerial view of Gateway Farm showing the lane Rosco traveled, the pond where Big Blue lived and the forest surrounding the farm. Photo credit to J.T. Calhoun.

Ginger
Leader of the Gateway Posse. Photo taken by the author.

Big Blue's Home At Gateway Farm. Photo taken by the author.

Rosco Crying From The Wasp, "Red Demons" Stings.
Photo taken by the author.

Rosco On The Lawn After Eating The Beans. Photo taken by the author.

Rosco Hiding On His Porch
After His Encounter With The Mother Goose. Photo
taken by the author.

The Gateway Posse Returns From Battling The Coyotes In The Snow. Photo taken by the author.

Rosco is On His Mat In The Laundry Room. Photo taken by the author.

Big Blue's View of Ken & Ms. Trudy's House from The Big Pond At Gateway. Photo taken by the author.

Rosco By Ms. Trudy's Chair. Photo taken by the author.

A blue catfish like Big Blue.

Ken Captures Big Blue. The photo was taken by Ms. Trudy shortly after Ken caught Big Blue.

Collins, *The Pirate,* as a puppy.
Photograph taken at Gateway by the author.

A masked bandit like Ralph

The Posse deals with a serpent during their patrol of Gateway Farm

Actual Photograph of the posse killing a serpent they found in the childrens' playground area of Gateway Farm. Credit to Leah Calhoun.

Ken and Trudy Bangs
Photo credit to Fresh Wind Photography, Texarkana, Texas.

**Other Books By Ken Bangs**

**Available From Amazon**

Arctic Warriors

Guardians In Blue

Guardians In Blue ~ Book Two

The Adventurous Travels of Miranda & J-Dog

Out of Saul ~ Paul
*From Tarsus to Aquae Salviae*

*Moses, Prince of Egypt ~ Son of Abraham*

*Daniel, Historian & Prophet*

*Ken Bangs Writing*

www.ingramcontent.com/pod-product-compliance
Lightning Source LLC
LaVergne TN
LVHW010618100826
845148LV00014B/3023

* 9 7 8 1 7 3 3 1 1 9 4 2 9 *